The Diary of Janie Ray

Books 6 & 7

The Case of the Missing Medallion

And

What Do People Wear in the Future, Anyway?

By Lila Segal

The Case of the Missing Medallion

♥ May 13, 2011 ♥

You know how sometimes, when something bad happens, you wake up in the morning and it takes you a few seconds to remember that something's wrong?

Well, that's what happened to me this morning. For the first blissful moments after I opened my eyes, I looked out the window and sighed contentedly. The sun was shining, the birds were chirping, and a warm and peaceful feeling settled over me.

Then it hit me like a punch in the stomach, and I sat up abruptly, feeling the blood drain from my face.

The medallion was missing!!

I had stayed up until after midnight, searching every corner of my room and the clubhouse. I even emptied my desk drawers, dumping the contents on the floor and combing through them, and looked through all the pockets of my dirty laundry. It was really gone.

I jumped out of bed and changed into jeans and a tee shirt, quickly brushing my teeth and racing downstairs. I'm very picky about brushing my teeth – I hate having bad breath, and I can't stand the way my mouth feels in the morning before I brush. If there's ever a zombie apocalypse, I'll probably be the girl who gets eaten because she can't run away before making a stop in the bathroom!

"Hi, Janie!" my mom called out cheerfully when she saw me.

"Where's RJ?" I asked, so lost in my thoughts that I didn't even acknowledge her. If the medallion wasn't in my room, RJ's room was the next place I'd look. He's always peeking in through my door, and I know he's dying to get his little hands on my stuff!

"Hi Mom," my mom answered, raising an eyebrow at me. "I'm so glad to see you, Mom! Good morning, Mom!" My mom has a thing about polite greetings. If I come into the house and forget to say hi or whatever, she gets really annoyed.

I went over and gave her a quick hug. "Sorry, Mom. It's just -" My voice broke and I felt the sobs coming on.

"Janie, what is it?" She turned around to face me, a worried look on her face.

"My medallion! I lost it!"

My mom frowned. "What medallion, honey?"

I sniffed and took a deep breath, trying to stop myself from crying. *Janie, get a grip*, I thought. *Becoming hysterical is going to get you nowhere.* I steadied my voice. "The one I found in Florida, when I was seven!"

My mom gave me a puzzled look. Obviously, she had no idea what I was talking about, and she was probably thinking it was pretty strange for an eleven-year-old to be crying over some old souvenir!

She patted my head. "Don't worry, Janie, I'm sure it's here somewhere! Close your eyes and think back where you had it last. That usually works a lot better than just looking in random places."

My mom should know – she's *forever* losing stuff, especially her keys. Once she left her wallet in the grocery store, and we spent all day looking for it! Finally, after she gave up and cancelled all her credit cards, somebody called from the store and said she could come pick it up. "That's Murphy's Law," she had said, shaking her head. At first I thought Murphy's Law was some kind of rule about returning things that are lost, but it turns out that's just an expression grown-ups use when things go wrong, like someone calling to return your wallet right *after* you cancelled your credit cards. Personally, I think if you're going to lose your wallet, you shouldn't complain if someone returns it, even if it takes a few hours!

"I looked everywhere, even in my hamper! I want to look in RJ's room. I'll bet he took it."

"I did not!" I hadn't even noticed RJ, sitting right there at the table in his pajamas, eating gluten-free toast. He looked as indignant as someone can be with Nutella all over their face. "And you can't go into my room, anyway, remember?"

I sighed. I never told you about the family meeting we had a couple of weeks ago. It was after I complained to my mom for the seventeen millionth time about RJ coming into my room and messing up my stuff. My parents are big on having family meetings to Talk About Our Problems. It wasn't such a big deal, but the bottom line is, we made a rule that RJ and I can't go into each other's rooms without permission. Which is a great idea, in theory. Or rather – it *would* be, if RJ ever remembered it when he wanted to go into *my* room.

"RJ," I said calmly, "I lost something very important, and I need to look for it. Can I please go into your room?"

RJ shook his head smugly. "Nope. Just like you didn't let me in yesterday."

I clenched my fists, trying not to show how mad I was. "I know I didn't, I'm sorry – next time I'll let you!"

He looked up at me eagerly. "Promise?" He had such a hopeful expression on his face that I felt like a real jerk. The little guy really looks up to me, even if he is a pain most of the time.

I reached out and tweaked his nose. "Promise."

"Ok, you can go in. But I didn't take it!" He took a big bite out of his toast, waited a few seconds and opened his mouth so I could see the chewed-up food.

"Gross!" I shrieked. But my expression softened. "I don't think you took it on purpose," I said. "But I just have to make sure it isn't in there."

******

I searched RJ's room for almost an hour before I had to leave for school. I didn't find the medallion, but I *did* find a Barbie that's been missing for almost a year and one of my favorite bracelets! RJ's lucky I'm way too upset about the medallion right now to care about other stuff.

I walked to school slowly, the knot in the pit of my stomach growing larger. This was nothing short of a disaster. Leave it to me to be the first Bearer of the Medallion to actually lose the darn thing! I couldn't even begin to imagine what the implications of this might be.

I didn't *want* to imagine.

I tried to think back to the last time I had used the medallion, going over and over the events in my mind. It was when we had gone to see Never Say Never, and I went back in time to fix the whole being-late-and-lying-to-my-parents fiasco. After that, I had decided to hide it in my closet and not use it again, until I figured out what I was *supposed* to do with it. And I'm 100% sure I never took it out after that! So it's not like I could have left it somewhere or anything.

When I got to school, Sheila was standing by the blackboard, talking to Calvin. She was giggling at something, throwing her head back and looking very interested in what he was saying. I shook my head. Did she even know how ridiculous she looked? If she was trying to hide the fact that she had a MASSIVE crush on Calvin, she wasn't doing a very good job.

"Sorry, Calvin," I said, smiling apologetically. "I need to borrow Sheila for a minute." I grabbed her arm and dragged her into the bathroom.

"What the heck was that all about?" Sheila sputtered, straightening her shirt and looking at me like I had fallen from Mars. Ever since Calvin started hanging out with us, Sheila's been kind of dressing up for school. Like blow-drying her hair in the morning and wearing nicer shirts and stuff. Which, if you ask me, is pretty weird. I have to admit, Calvin's probably the cutest guy in our grade, but she acts all silly every time she talks to him, and it's really starting to get on my nerves.

I looked around to make sure the bathroom was empty. "The medallion!" I whispered loudly. "It's gone!"

"What do you mean, it's gone?" Sheila whispered back. Then she spoke in a regular voice. "And why are you whispering? Nobody's in here."

She had a point.

"I mean, it's gone! It isn't in my closet, and I've looked *everywhere* in my room and in the clubhouse. It's not there!"

Her eyes widened, and she just kind of stood there, looking at me. "Oh, no," she finally said.

"Oh no, indeed." I shook my head.

****

Somehow we made it through the morning, and at lunch we found a table in the far corner of the cafeteria. Kellie was home preparing for the Starbright Showdown – it's tomorrow, remember!?? And Alexis had a dentist's appointment. Which was lucky, because we couldn't talk about the medallion in front of them.

"We have to think about this logically," Sheila was saying. She twirled spaghetti around on her fork before taking a small bite and making a face. "Ugh. You know, the fact that they can mess up something as simple as spaghetti and meatballs is kind of a feat of nature, isn't it."

Leave it to Sheila to think about *food* at a time like this. "Actually, what's a feat of nature is that you can think about spaghetti when the world is coming to an end!"

"Sorry." She put her fork down. "Well, except for me and your family, who's been in your room recently?"

"Nobody -" I started to say, and then I stopped. Well, Kellie and Alexis had been there, but I couldn't imagine they would have taken anything. And -

"Oh, hi Marcia!" Sheila interrupted my thoughts.

And Marcia. Of course.

"Hi Sheila! Hi Janie!" Marcia was balancing her tray with one hand and waving to us with the other. She sat down across from Sheila and gave us a huge smile. "Mind if I sit with you guys? I had classroom duty, so I haven't even started eating yet!"

Sheila and I looked at each other. Just a couple of days ago, the idea of Marcia – A.K.A MTS or Marcia the Snob – eating lunch with us was pretty much unthinkable. She was queen of the "in crowd" and most definitely NOT my friend. She was the one who made up the whole "Janie the Frizz" business, and she never missed an opportunity to call Kellie "Kellie Smelly". If we had asked to eat lunch with her and her crew of princesses, they probably would have laughed us out the cafeteria.

But ever since Kellie was on Starbright, Marcia's been trying really hard to become our friend. I'm still not sure I trust her, but Alexis – who's been friends with Marcia since they were little – wants us to give her a chance.

A couple of days ago MTS even came over to my house! And – you guessed it - she's the other person who was in my room. But she was only there for a few seconds. And I really don't think she took the medallion. First of all – when I came in, I saw her standing there and staring at the fire safety poster I got during our class trip. She wasn't rummaging through my closet or anything, and she didn't look the least bit suspicious! And second of all – she's trying *really* hard to get us to like her right now. Why would she risk losing all her new friends just to take some old medallion?

"Sure," I said, moving my tray back to make room for Marcia's. "Have a seat. We were just trying to figure out how the cafeteria could ruin something as basic as spaghetti." I took a bite. Wow, Sheila was right – it was rubbery *and* mushy. Which if you think about it, is quite an accomplishment. Yuck.

"Yeah, I know." Marcia started picking at the soggy green stuff that was supposed to be salad. "So!" she said brightly, changing the subject. "What are you guys doing this summer? My family's going to Italy for two weeks! And after that, I'm going to sleepaway camp for a whole month!" She brushed a few strands of hair out of her eyes.

I studied her. She was wearing a yellow short-sleeved shirt, a silver and black necklace that looked very exotic, and designer jeans. And somehow, even though it was only May, she was already tanned. It *figured* she'd have a completely fabulous summer planned.

"Um, I actually don't have any plans yet." I've been going to horseback riding camp since I was nine, but I told my parents I'm definitely not going back this year. The counselors are horrible. And the other kids all know each other from school. I love horses, but not enough to spend all day with kids who barely talk to me. Plus, the camp is very disorganized. Once we went on a three-hour ride and the counselors forgot to bring water! When we said we were thirsty, they told us to drink our spit. Which, besides being incredibly gross, doesn't actually make you less thirsty. And they acted like it was our fault! My parents called the camp director to complain, but I doubt it made much of a difference. I'm thinking maybe tennis camp. Or creative writing camp, if I can convince one of my friends to come with me!"

Marcia nodded, and I could tell she was making a big effort not to look smug. She looked at Sheila. "What about you?"

"I'm going to my grandparents' house for a couple of weeks, and then I don't know."

"Oh," Marcia said. "Well, maybe we can all find a day to get together when I get back from Italy! I'm leaving the day after school ends. We'll be in Rome for a whole week, and then we're going to a horse farm in the north!"

"Wow," Sheila said wistfully. "That's awesome. I'm so jealous."

"Yeah," I said, raising an eyebrow at her. "We never go *anywhere*."

****

After school, Sheila came over so we could make a game plan. We *have* to find the medallion before tomorrow night! We all got tickets to go see Kellie in the Starbright Showdown, and I don't see how I'll be able to concentrate on the show if the medallion is still missing!

If you want to hear about how I used the medallion to help Kellie get on Starbright, I wrote all about that whole business in earlier parts of the diary – so check it out, if you're interested. When she first came to Middlestar Elementary, Kellie was the most unpopular kid in our class, and everyone made fun of her. But that feels like ancient history. She has the best singing voice I ever heard, and if she wins tomorrow, she may be able to make her own album with a real production company!

"So where else can we look?" Sheila asked, lying back on my bed. "Are you sure it's not in your closet?" She gestured to the mess that was spilling out onto the floor. "It's not exactly the easiest place to find things."

"Yes, I'm sure. But I guess it can't hurt to look one more time."

Just as we finished dumping all my clothes out onto the floor, there was a knock on the door, and my mom peeked in.

"Hi girls, I thought maybe you'd want -" She stopped and stared at the huge mess on the floor. "What are you guys doing?"

"Oh, we're just -"

"We're sorting through Janie's clothes for the summer," Sheila interjected.

"Well, that's a very good idea!" my mom nodded approvingly. She handed us a plate of veggies. "I thought maybe you guys would want a snack. I have to do an errand, and RJ's coming with me. Oh – and if you're already sorting your clothes, maybe you could organize your closet while you're at it. It's always such a mess!"

Sheila stifled a giggle and I smiled. Ever since our little trip back to 1985, it's been hard to take my mom's pronouncements about my slovenliness quite as seriously. And I'll bet you know what I'm about to say: If you want to find out more about *that*, you can read earlier parts of my diary…

As we folded the last couple of shirts and put them back on the shelf, I let out a disheartened sigh. Obviously, searching the same places over and over again would get us nowhere.

"What about your desk?" Sheila asked.

"Nah, I dumped everything out last night," I shook my head. "There really isn't any point in doing it again."

"Well," Sheila said, ignoring me and opening my top drawer. "Sometimes it helps for someone else to look. Remember when I lost my necklace?"

A few months ago, Sheila went bananas when she couldn't find this genuine gold necklace she got from her grandmother when she was born. She didn't talk about anything else for almost a week. She thought she had looked everywhere, but finally her mom went through her dresser, and there it was, right between two pairs of shorts.

"Well, that's different," I said, closing the drawer. "I'm telling you, it isn't there!"

Sheila snorted and leaned back on the bed. "Fine, have it your way." Then, out of nowhere, she jumped up and shrieked. "I've got it!"

"What?!" I was getting annoyed.

"Well, remember the letters you got from your older self? Maybe you should write yourself a letter and ask for help! I'll bet Prof. Janie Ray will be able to tell you just where to find the medallion!"

I bit my fingernail, considering what she said. I had to admit, that was a pretty good idea. "Ok," I said slowly, sitting down at my desk and taking out a pen and paper. "Let's write a draft, and then I'll translate it into our secret language."

You already know what I'm going to say, so I won't bother. Yup, earlier parts of the diary. Plus, I've pasted our secret language into the back of the diary, so that I won't lose it. So you can look back there if you have no idea what I'm talking about.

I quickly finished the note and read it to Sheila.

Dear Prof. Janie Ray,

Hi, it's me again. Or rather, you. I have a huge problem. I can't find the medallion! I hope you remember when this happened, so that you can tell me where to look. I'm desperate!

Love, Janie

"Ok," Sheila said, when I had finished copying it over in our secret code. "Let's hide it in your closet, where we put the other ones. Hopefully, she'll answer right away, like she did last time!"

I folded the note and stuffed it into the little crevice at the back of my closet. The last time I'd communicated with my older self, her answers had appeared almost instantaneously under the pillow on my bed. I guess she could just use the medallion to travel back to the exact right moment and leave them for me.

After a few tense seconds passed, I got up and felt around under my pillow.

"Anything there?" Sheila's voice was stiff.

"Nope." I sat down on my bed and waited, checking every few seconds to see whether anything had arrived.

"Maybe she's just busy," Sheila offered, sounding uncertain.

"I don't think so," I frowned. "Even if it takes her years to write back, she can still travel back to the exact right time to give us the answer. From our point of view, it should still be instantaneous."

"Right…" Sheila's voice trailed off. Then she reached again for my desk drawer. "What about the key you got from your Grandpa? The one we used to open the vault at the bank?"

My heart started racing and I felt another wave of panic coming on. "What about it? It should be right in here." I pushed in front of her and started frantically rummaging through the top desk drawer. I had been keeping the key in my desk, but I hadn't thought to notice whether it was there when I searched through it the night before. "Come on, it's got to - Oh, thank goodness, here it is." I grabbed the key and held onto it, slowing letting out a sigh of relief. My heart was still pounding. If the key had gone missing too, we'd really be in trouble.

As I started closing the drawer, Sheila stuck her hand in. "Wait, what's that?" She pulled out three pink notes that had been under the key.

"Those are the old notes from my older self, why?"

"Well, look at them!" Sheila turned around and shoved them in my face.

I turned the notes over in my hand, my mouth hanging open. They were there, but they looked like Swiss cheese, like a little kid had attacked them with a hole puncher. I could barely even see the words.

My first thought was – RJ! I can't believe that little brat came into my room *again* and messed up my stuff!!

But then I remembered – our hole puncher has been broken for ages. I've been bugging my mom to get a new one, but she keeps forgetting. Plus – the notes were just where I left them, and it really didn't look like anyone had touched them. I highly doubted RJ would come into my room, punch holes into pieces of paper, and then just put them back exactly where he had found them. That really didn't make sense.

Something was happening, and I needed to find out what - before things got completely out of control.

****

Without another word, I dropped the key into my pocket and started walking quickly towards the stairs. Sheila jumped up and followed me. "Hey, Janie, where are you -"

"To the vault," I said. "I can't believe I didn't think of this before! If we're going to find any clues about what's going on, it's going to be in the vault." I scribbled a quick note to my mom to tell her we were going riding, and headed out the front door.

We got on our bikes and rode quickly in the direction of the bank, not even stopping at Starbucks this time. As we turned onto Crawley Street, Sheila pulled out her phone and looked at the time. "It's already five," she said anxiously. "We'll only have about an hour."

We pedaled faster, and a few minutes later, we pulled up in front of the bank. Sheila got off her bike and took out her inhaler. I've mentioned she has asthma, right? When we were little, it was pretty bad, and she even had to go to the hospital a few times! Now she only gets attacks once in a while, but she has to carry an inhaler with her all the time. Which, as you might remember, does come in handy sometimes.

"You ok?"

"Yeah." She leaned forward with her hands on her knees and took several deep breaths. Then she straightened up. "Ok. Let's go."

I nodded and wiped my forehead with my hand. I wasn't very out of breath, but it was hot, and I was sweating.

This time, I looked forward to the burst of cool air as we opened the door of the bank and walked inside. It still felt weird to be going to the bank without a grown-up, but not as weird as it did the first time.

Once inside, Sheila headed straight for the bowl of Jolly Rancher candies in the middle of the lobby. Before I could say anything, she turned around and made a face at me. "They wouldn't have candy here if they didn't want people to take it!" she whispered indignantly. "Here, have a sour apple one." She tossed it at me, and I caught it, shaking my head and smiling.

"Come on," I said, giving Sheila's sleeve a gentle tug. "Michael's in his office."

Michael's the bank manager, and he's also the person in charge of keeping watch over the vault where the secret Histories are kept. He's part of what Grandpa Charlie called "The Outer Circle" – people who are there to help the Bearer of the Medallion at critical junctures, but who don't know all the details of what the medallion really does.

As we walked towards his office, my eyes were drawn to the strange inscription on the wall of the bank, the one that gave me the shock of my life the last time we were here.

It said:

Jki usdy ziolus quz jeti el lu jkoj ixizyjkesn muils'j kowwis oj usri

I'm sure you can figure out what that means.

My heart lurched as I was suddenly struck by a very disturbing thought: The last time we were here, Michael told us the inscription was a quote by Albert Einstein, and that it was given to the bank in 1933. Well, if Michael knew what the inscription said, that meant he knew our secret language, or at least could figure it out! And how many other people saw that inscription every day and maybe knew what it meant?

"Janie, Sheila, how nice to see you!" Michael's voice broke into my thoughts even before we had a chance to knock on his door. "Please, come in." He ushered us into his office.

We sat down at his big mahogany desk, and once again he poured us two glasses of lemonade. I guess the bike ride must have made me thirsty, because my throat suddenly felt extremely dry, and I began gulping down the juice as if my life depended on it. When I was finished, I put the glass back down on the table and wiped my mouth on my sleeve.

I looked around the elegant office, and for the first time I noticed that in addition to the life-size portrait of an old man that I now knew covered the secret door to the vault, the walls were covered in lots of smaller paintings. The rug was dark blue and shaggy, and a wooden banister reached across the back wall, covered in tiny inscriptions I couldn't make out.

I cleared my throat, wondering fleetingly if I should tell Michael about the missing medallion. I remembered Grandpa Charlie's warning to avoid asking Michael too many questions, and decided not to. It would be best not take any chances.

"Um, thank you for the lemonade," I said, clearing my throat again. I reached into my pocket and took out the key. "We would like to spend some time in the vault today."

Michael smiled and picked up the key, "Not a problem, girls. I'll just let you in and you can take all the time you need." He glanced at his clock and added apologetically, "Or at least until six. That's when we close today."

He moved aside the big, life-size portrait to once again reveal a huge, digital combination lock. He punched in the code and the door swung open.

Once Sheila and I were alone, she sat down at the small table in the center of the room and gave me a look. "Ok, we're here now." She gestured to the bookshelves that covered the walls. "Where do we start? And what exactly are we looking for?"

"Good question," I murmured. I walked over to the shelf in the bottom corner of the room, and bent down. 1995-2011. I picked up the most recent notebook, the one that had 2011 scrawled across it in red marker, and started leafing through it. The entries I had seen the last time were still there: March 2011, Janie returns home; April 2011, Janie uses medallion to help Kellie win Starbright. I flipped ahead to the future entry I had seen, hardly daring to breathe: August 12, 2011, Janie takes first trip as Bearer of the Medallion.

My face went white as the implications of what I was seeing sunk in: Like Prof. Janie Ray's letters, the entry was full of holes.

****

I slumped into the chair across from Sheila and put my head down on my hands. I was starting to despair.

"What, Janie? What did you see?" For the first time since this whole thing started, Sheila looked really worried.

"The future entries are full of holes, just like the notes from my future self! Which I guess means -"

"What?"

"I'm not completely sure, but I think it means the medallion is really gone. Everything that depends on me having the medallion in the future is slowly disappearing. If I don't have the medallion,

I can't take my first journey as Bearer! And if my future self doesn't have it, she can't answer us."

"Yeah, but-" Sheila was picking off the maroon nail polish she had started wearing the past few weeks. "We've already *gotten* notes from your future self. Which means she must have gotten the medallion somehow. And if she eventually *did* get the medallion, she should be able to answer us now, too. It doesn't make sense."

I bit my lip. "A lot of this doesn't make sense. The other day I did some research about time travel on the internet, and all the books that have ever been written about it are full of paradoxes that seem unsolvable. Like the Grandfather Paradox."

Sheila made a puzzled face. "The Grandfather Paradox?"

"You know, if someone goes back in time and kills their grandfather."

"Why would they do something stupid like that?" Sheila snorted.

I giggled. "It's just an example. If they kill their grandfather, they'll never be born, right? And if they're never born, they can't go back and kill their grandfather. It's an endless circle. All I know," my voice got serious, "is that what happens now seems to affect the future, even *if* the future has already changed the past."

Sheila was nodding. "Ok. So things are disappearing. But what are we supposed to do now? We seem to have reached a dead end."

"Yeah..." *Maybe we should start by reading some Histories*, I thought. I looked around and shuddered – the sheer quantity of books was daunting.

Where should we start? And what should we be looking for?

I got up and walked over to the shelves that contained the earlier Histories, stopping when I saw one that said 1300-1200 BC. "Hey, look!" I turned to Sheila. "These are the Histories from the period of Ramses the Great, when Grandpa Charlie said the medallion was first created. And that's where we went that time to rescue my mom, remember?" I bent down and picked up one of the old manuscripts. It was much older and more brittle than the one from 2011, and it had 1279 BC inscribed across the front. I placed it gently on the table, praying it wouldn't crumble to dust.

"1279 was the year we travelled to, remember?"

Sheila rolled her eyes. "No. I forgot. Of course I remember, banana brain! But why should we start with this one?"

I shrugged. "We have to start somewhere. Got any better ideas?"

Sheila shook her head. "I guess not."

With trembling hands, I opened the manuscript and started turning the pages. I inhaled sharply as I realized that I could read it, even though it was written in a strange language that looked like Hieroglyphics. You know, the picture writing that was used in ancient Egypt? It was just like when we travelled back to rescue my mom, and we could understand everything that people were saying, even though they were speaking a strange and very foreign language. I shuddered again as I began to read aloud.

****

This morning I finished my lesson in just under an hour. Senmut is usually very strict, and he doesn't have any patience for my tricks - but today I could tell even he was amused when I hid under the bed to avoid studying. I already know how to write, and I'm very good at it, so I don't understand why I have to waste my time with lessons!

Sheila and I looked at each other and grinned. School: Boring Kids Since 1200 BC.

When I was finally finished, Nefertiti and I went to play in the River. It was such a hot day! We weren't supposed to be there, though. While we were splashing around, I suddenly heard footsteps and we hid between the reeds. If Senmut caught us here by ourselves, we'd probably get whipped!

This was interesting and all, but it didn't seem like it was going to help us. I flipped ahead several pages and continued reading.

Today we learned about The Great Disaster, the terrible famine that nearly destroyed our country more than a hundred years ago! The grownups mention it sometimes, but I never really knew what they were talking about. It was at the time of my Ancestor, Amenhotep III.

Her ancestor? Who was writing this?

There was a terrible famine for seven whole years, and everyone would have probably died if Amenhotep hadn't had a dream that foretold the catastrophe. His closest advisor was a dream interpreter, and he told him to prepare for the famine by stocking a huge amount of grain, enough to sustain the entire population for over a decade.

As Senmut told me the story, my heart swelled with pride. If it weren't for my Ancestors, Egypt would have been destroyed!

A chill went through me and I looked up at Sheila.

"T-t-this is- "

"Yup." Sheila was nodding, a shocked expression on her face.

I went back to reading, suddenly wishing I had paid more attention in Sunday School. *This was just like the story of Joseph and the Pharaoh, from the Bible!*

After my lesson, I went to find Nefertiti, and something very disturbing happened. I had to go through the west side of the palace to reach her room, and on the way I passed through the room they are rebuilding for next year's Festival. There were planks of wood and mud bricks everywhere, and ten or twelve slaves were carrying in various materials from outside. All of a sudden, one of them fell to the ground, moaning and holding his side. And instead of helping him, the palace guard hit him with his whip and yelled at him to stand up. I hid behind the doorway and held my breath. It's a lucky thing nobody saw me, I could have gotten in lots of trouble for being there! And now I don't know if I should tell anyone what I saw.

I flipped even further ahead in the manuscript.

Senmut says that knowledge is a very valuable thing, but sometimes I wish I could forget the things that I know. When

I was little, I was so carefree and everything seemed so peaceful. I could play for hours in the palace, eating grapes and dates and making dolls out of whatever materials I could find.

I was so innocent then. And now that I know what's really going on, nothing is the same. I can barely even bring myself to look at my mother. How can she go on, living this life and pretending everything's fine? When I was a young child, she used to hold me on her lap for hours and sing to me, and I wanted nothing more than to grow up and be just like her. Now I wonder how I can even live in the same house as she does.

Our whole lives are built on lies. Lies and the horrible, evil suffering of all the millions of people we have enslaved. Millions of people who think my father is a god! My heart is full of bitterness.

After Senmut told me about The Great Disaster, I became curious and read some of the official histories of that time. Official histories that are hidden in the palace, and available only to the Pharaoh and his family. Yes, it is true that Amenhotep saved the people from famine and certain destruction. But he did so at a terrible price. He distributed grain to thousands of people, but he used their hunger to enslave them, to take their property and ultimately their freedom.

I always grew up with slaves and it seemed like part of the natural course of things. Like Bakt, who practically raised me and always had a kind word when I fell down or got hurt. I never thought about the fact that she was taken from her family when she was just a little girl. She never had a mommy! My heart fills with tears when I think about how much she must have suffered.

That is the problem with knowledge. Now that my eyes have been opened, they can never be closed again.

I took a deep breath and turned the page again.

Last night I had a dream that shook me to my core. I was going through my mother's basket of jewelry, her gold chains and precious gemstones dripping between my fingers, when I suddenly came across a large, round pendant. It was flat and black, and almost the size of a small pomegranate. And the strange thing was, it had my name on it: Bithiah. I woke with a start, my heart pounding. And I realized – this was no ordinary dream, but a message I was meant to understand. I waited until my mother went out and slipped into her room. I found the basket and was overcome by a wistful feeling, as I remembered the many, long happy days I spent dressing up in her clothes and trying on her jewelry as a little kid. The basket looked just like it did in the dream, and I was not surprised when I found the odd, round pendant with my name on it. I grasped onto it and quickly hid it under the folds of my dress. This medallion is a magic one, of that I am certain. Now I just have to figure out what it does.

My voice caught. She was talking about the medallion!

I went back to my room and hid the pendant carefully. I had just a few minutes to get to my lesson, or Senmut would come looking for me. But just then, I heard my mother's low voice outside my window. I crouched down and kept silent, straining to hear what she was saying. As I have learned, in a place so full of secrets as this palace, information is gold. And then I realized - she was talking about me!

"Bithiah hasn't been herself lately," my mother was saying, her voice worried.

"Yes, I have noticed." It was my Aunt Kemanut, Nefertiti's mother, who answered her.

"She seems so sad, so withdrawn. And sometimes I see a gleam in her eye, like she has nothing but contempt for me. I have tried to be a good mother. What have I done wrong?"

"Kiya, it is not your fault," Kemanut answered softly. "All young girls go through this phase. Remember when we were girls? And you started refusing to wear any clothes that resembled our mother's? It is but natural."

"No, this is something different. And yesterday she said something that worried me terribly. I had ordered Bakt to prepare a snack for Anen, and Bithiah was making a terrible face. When I asked her what was wrong, she said it was a shame Bakt never got to know her own mother!"

Kemanut gasped. "Why would she say something like that?"

There was silence. Then my mother said, "Bithiah has always been a very kind person, with a generous heart. And I love her for that. But each person has their destiny. And it is our destiny to rule and Bakt's destiny to serve. Bithiah should be old enough to understand that!"

Their voices grew fainter as they began walking towards the palace courtyard, and I stayed where I was, thinking about what my mother had said. I most certainly was old enough. Old enough to understand that it should be no one's "destiny" to serve.

Sheila broke in. "Wow. That's incredible. Pharaoh's daughter was against slavery! Wait – was she the one who adopted Moses?"

"I don't know," I mused. I couldn't get over the fact that I was reading the diary of someone who lived at the time of the Pharaohs! If it hadn't been for everything that had happened over the past few weeks, I never would have believed it.

Obviously.

"Well, as interesting as this is," Sheila said, "I'm not sure how it's going to help us find the medallion."

"Yeah," I agreed. "But you've got to admit it's fascinating. This is the history of the beginning of the medallion! Let's read just a bit more, and then we can look through some more stuff."

"Ok," Sheila settled in her chair like she was getting ready to hear a good story. "Keep on reading. But skip ahead a little."

> *It has finally all become clear to me. The whole horrifying picture. And today, for the first time, I shared my knowledge with Nefertiti. She was her usual skeptical self, but once I showed her what the medallion can do, she stopped making little sarcastic comments and was much more cooperative.*

"They had sarcasm in Ancient Egypt?" Sheila asked suddenly.

"Well, why not?" I answered. "They were people, just like us, weren't they?"

"I don't know, it just seems weird." She sniffed.

> *The medallion is the one thing I can use to stand up to the terrible injustices I see around me. My family rules through deception and cunning. We use disasters — like the famine —*

30

to gain control, and we maintain it through a web of lies. The medallion offers some small hope for the future, if only I can use it to prevent the kinds of catastrophes that enable my family to gain more and more control. And if only I can use it to do small things, even insignificant ones, to help bring freedom to some of the enslaved. It will not be an easy task. But I must try.

And now that Nefertiti knows what's going on, I will not be alone.

Today something else finally became clear. Several months ago, on the very day my father ascended the throne, a strange girl suddenly appeared in the midst of the festivities. She was dressed very oddly, and she looked completely out of place. Everyone thought she was some kind of Goddess or Evil Spirit, and my father had her locked up.

But then more strangers came, and they all disappeared, escaping my father's clutches. At the time, I didn't give it much thought — events that appear to be magical are not such an unusual thing. My father has a whole cadre of magicians, who work day and night to create the illusion of magical power - just one of the many illusions my family uses to control the people. But Father took something from the stranger that day, and it is only now that I understand what it was — a medallion, just like the one I found!

And now I cannot help but wonder — could the stranger have been a visitor from the future?

I gasped as thoughts whirled around in my head. This daughter of a Pharaoh was describing my mother! And was the medallion she found the same one Ramses had taken from us? I put my hand on my forehead and massaged my temples – I was starting to get a headache.

I closed the manuscript and put it carefully back on the shelf, stretching my legs and scanning the other notebooks that lay beside it. I picked up another one, with 1270 BC written across the front, and opened it to a random page.

> *I have become a prisoner to deception. Every day I wake up feeling like an actress in one of the plays we watch at our Festivals. I put on a contented, friendly face and go about my daily activities, while all along I'm burning inside.*
>
> *Desperate to maintain power over those he has enslaved, my father has been issuing one absurd decree after another. Today he ordered all male slave children to be killed while they are still babies! One cannot imagine a greater horror. And yet the people still worship him, still treat him as a god.*

Sheila whispered, "It *is* the Pharaoh from the Bible!"

I nodded mutely, the panicky feeling beginning to rise again in my throat. "How much time do we have left?" I asked, surprised by how shaky my voice sounded.

Sheila glanced at her phone. "About twenty minutes."

I reluctantly closed the manuscript and put it down, walking back to the corner of the room and picking up the most recent History.

"What are you doing? Didn't we already look at that one?"

"Just a second, I want to see something." I flipped forward to the future entry about my first trip as Bearer of the Medallion, and was dismayed once again to see that it was still full of holes. If anything, there were *more* of them. But as I turned the page, I smiled to myself. The previous future entries were disappearing, but there were new ones! Maybe they would give us an idea of what was going on.

I studied the page, my pulse quickening. Unlike the entry about my future trip, this one remained fully intact. And it was somehow different. The handwriting looked like that of a young girl – full of loops, and hearts over the "i"s instead of dots. It looked oddly... familiar.

I handed the notebook to Sheila. "Can you read a bit?"

She knit her eyebrows and stared at the page. "Wow, this looks like it was written by a kid!" She started to read.

> *Jackie's been acting really weird. On the weekends she's home from college, she spends all her time in her room with the door closed, watching videos on her computer. And she almost never leaves the house! But she's being really nice to me for a change, going out of her way to pay attention to me. And since Mom and Dad are almost never home, she's been making dinner a lot.*
>
> *I still don't understand why she wanted Janie's medallion so badly. When I asked her, she just said she would explain later. But she promised me that once she did, I would understand why it was so important.*

A shock went through my body, and I practically fell over on my chair. Sheila stopped reading, her hands visibly trembling, and we stared at each other wordlessly for what seemed like a long time.

"Go on," I said urgently. "We don't have much longer."

> *Last night I went into her room while she was taking a bath, just to borrow one of her barrettes. Her computer was on, and I couldn't resist taking a peek at the screen. I didn't mean to snoop or anything, but an email was open, and I could see it had something to do with the medallion. So I read it. I'm the one who got her the stupid medallion, so I have the right to find out what all the fuss is about, right?*
>
> *The subject of the email was "Protectors of Fate", and it was signed by someone who called himself The Privileged. How weird, right?*
>
> *I didn't have time to read the whole thing, but one line stuck in my mind: "We must strive to allow fate to take its course, and we must stand in the way of those who seek to use the Medallion to interfere in history's plans". I didn't really understand what it meant, but Jackie was right - it did sound pretty important!*

Just then, there came a knock on the door, and I could hear Michael's muffled voice calling us from outside the vault. "Three minutes, girls. We're closing up for the day."

We left the bank in silence, so lost in thought that it took me three tries to reach the right combination on my bike lock. The Privileged? And The Protectors of Fate? This was beginning to be too much, even for me.

And something else was bothering me, something I couldn't quite put my finger on. *Who was Jackie?*

I took off my scrunchie, gathered my hair back into a ponytail, and put on my helmet. Reason number 256 I hate my frizzy, curly hair: It's really, really hard to stuff it into a bicycle helmet.

"Ok," Sheila finally said as we got on our bikes and rode off. "So all we have to do is find some random person with an older sister named Jackie and steal the medallion back from them. Easy-peasy."

It sounded so absurd, I had to laugh. But inside, another knot had formed in the pit of my stomach. The medallion seemed to be further away than ever, and it didn't look like we were going to find it any time soon.

****

I got home to find RJ curled up on the living room couch listening to his mp3 player (what else??), and my dad preparing dinner. I let the door slam behind me and stomped into the kitchen.

"Hi Janie!" My dad called out cheerfully when he saw me.

"Hi," I answered glumly. "Where's Mom?" Automatically, I went to the refrigerator, opened it and started looking inside for something to eat.

"Gee, don't you seem happy to see me!" my dad said. I looked up, worried I'd insulted him, but he had a big smile on his face. "Mom's at the library, she's got deadline this week. What's wrong, sweetie? You seem upset."

The last thing I wanted to do was start explaining all about the medallion again. But it couldn't hurt to ask him if he'd seen it.

"No, I'm ok." I tried my best to look happy. Or at least, not to look horribly devastated. "I just spent all day looking for something really important I lost!"

"What is it?" Now he looked concerned.

"Um, just this medallion I found when we were in Florida a few years ago." Gee, now *both* my parents were going to think I'd lost my mind.

He frowned. "I don't think I know which medallion you're talking about. We can look for it together after dinner, if you want."

I shook my head. "No thanks, it's ok. Actually, I'm really tired." I covered my mouth and yawned really loudly. "I think I'm just gonna go to sleep now. I told Sheila I'd meet up with her in the morning."

******

♥ May 14, 2011 ♥

After closing the door to my room, the first thing I did was check the notes from Prof. Janie Ray. Sure enough, they were slowly disintegrating. I fought back tears as I changed into my pajamas, brushed my teeth and climbed into bed.

My sleep was fitful, and twice I jolted awake, sweating from nightmares I couldn't even remember. I jumped out of bed and turned on the light, my heart thumping in my chest. For a split second, I thought I was about to remember what it was about *Jackie* that was bugging me. But the thought slipped away before it was even able to form fully in my mind.

In the morning, I got up early and was in the kitchen having breakfast before my parents woke up. And they're definitely morning people, even on weekends. I looked at the clock. It was six-fifteen.

I made myself some scrambled eggs and poured a glass of orange juice. Now that I'm eleven, I'm allowed to make eggs and stuff by myself, as long as I make sure to turn off the stove when I'm done, and as long as I clean up after myself. Last Mother's Day we surprised my mom with pancakes and coffee in bed, and she was really happy. But when she came down to the kitchen afterwards, she said she almost had a heart attack when she saw how messy it was. Personally, I don't see what the big deal is - how can you cook without making a mess?

It was after I sat down at the table and took my first bite of egg that it hit me, like a ton of bricks falling on my head, and I nearly spit out my food.

Kellie had an older sister named Jackie.

****

I called Sheila right away, and we met at Greg's Coffee in the mall. It was the only place open this early on a Saturday that we could get to by bike.

"So you really think it was Kellie?" Sheila asked dubiously, taking a bite of her donut. We were both having cinnamon donuts and hot chocolate.

I shrugged, shaking my head. "I don't know what to think. I honestly can't imagine Kellie doing something like that. But it really looks like it, doesn't it?"

Sheila took a long drink of her cocoa before replying. "I can't imagine it either. And how would her writing get into the vault anyway? It's not like she has a key or anything."

"I don't know," I said, stirring my hot chocolate thoughtfully. "But there are a lot of things we don't know yet. How did any of the future entries get there? Michael said nobody's been in there for twenty-five years!"

"Ok," Sheila said after a while. "So maybe we should just call her."

I hesitated. Tonight was the Starbright Showdown! The last thing Kellie needed was for us to call her and distract her with all of this. On the other hand - maybe we could just call and wish her good luck. We didn't have to say anything, just see if she sounded weird or anything. "Ok. But don't mention anything that's going on."

Sheila rolled her eyes. "Of course not!" She pulled out her phone and dialed Kellie's number.

"Hi Mrs. Allen, this is Sheila. Is Kellie there?" She waited a few seconds. "Hi Kellie, it's Sheila! How are you doing?" There was another short silence and then, "Wow!! I'm here with Janie and we just wanted to wish you good luck tonight! We're so excited!" A few seconds later she passed the phone to me and whispered, "She sounds completely normal. She wants to talk to you, ok?"

I took the phone gingerly, thinking how strange it was that I was so nervous about talking to Kellie. "Hi Kellie!" I hoped she couldn't hear the strain in my voice.

"Hi Janie!" Kellie giggled. "I can't believe it's tonight!"

She *did* sound normal. But then again, if she *had* stolen the medallion, she'd obviously try and sound as normal as possible.

"I know! I'm really excited for you. Have you decided what to wear yet?" Kellie and her voice teacher had been debating whether she should wear the same regular clothes and clunky brown shoes she had worn the first time, or something snazzier.

"Yeah, we decided to go for what my voice teacher calls the 'regular kid look.' I actually feel more comfortable that way, and apparently it's part of my charm." She sighed.

"I'm sure you'll be amazing!" I said, trying to sound as enthusiastic as I would have been the day before. "And we'll be there cheering for you!"

"Thanks, Janie. I couldn't have done this without you. Literally." Kellie gave a short laugh. "Ok, well - I gotta go. My mom's standing over my head telling me to get off the phone."

I hung up and gave the phone back to Sheila." Well, that was helpful," I said with a wry smile. I dunked the rest of my donut in the hot chocolate and stuffed it into my mouth. Crisis or no crisis, this was *good*.

"Yeah." Just then, Sheila pointed at a table on the far side of the restaurant, near the door. "Look, it's Marcia and Jessica!" she exclaimed.

I turned around and groaned. The last thing I wanted right now was to talk to them. I glanced at the time on Sheila's phone. "What are they doing here so early? It's not even ten!"

Sheila shrugged, pushing her chair back. "I guess we should go say hello."

I stood up reluctantly. I still couldn't really get used to the idea that MTS was our friend.

Marcia and Jessica were sharing a big plate of pancakes with maple syrup and whipped cream. And Marcia was having what looked like a cappuccino. It so *figured* Marcia would be drinking coffee. My parents won't let me have coffee until I'm fifteen. Which is fine by me. Personally, I don't understand why people drink it. It's disgusting! My parents are completely addicted to it. My mom says she needs to have her coffee first thing in the morning to "feel like a person." And if she doesn't have any by noon, she gets a terrible headache!

Marcia was wearing a pink sweater and silver dangling earrings with little butterflies. Her hair was pulled back in a French braid, and I could have sworn she was wearing eye shadow. I really don't get the whole make-up business. Sheila wears lip gloss once in a while, especially these days. But it just makes me feel silly, like I'm wearing a costume. Plus, I don't even know if my mom would let me wear it.

Marcia saw us coming and waved, but Jessica just sat there glumly. I think she's worried we're going to steal Marcia away or something.

"Hi guys, you wanna come sit with us?" Marcia motioned to the chairs beside them.

"Uh… sure." Sheila answered before I had a chance to say anything. "We'll just go get our food."

We brought our stuff over and sat down at the table. Jessica still hadn't said anything, and was just sitting there stiffly, her arms crossed.

"So, are you guys going to Kellie's Starbright Showdown tonight?" Marcia asked.

"Yeah, of course! We wouldn't miss it." Sheila said. "And we even got backstage passes! We're going to be there when they interview Kellie and everything." Starbright always shows the contestants before and after their performances, hanging out with their friends and family or whoever came to cheer them on. Before all this losing the medallion stuff happened, I'd been really looking forward to being there.

"Wow, you're so lucky!" An envious note crept into Marcia's voice, but she was trying to make it seem like she didn't really care. Then she added casually, "Do you think she has any extra tickets?"

I looked at Sheila. "I don't know. Maybe you should ask her."

"I will!" She picked up her cup and took a sip. "Wow, this coffee is so good!"

I rolled my eyes and nudged Sheila under the table, trying to keep myself from laughing. This was SUCH typical Marcia-ness.

Sheila wrinkled her nose. "I don't like coffee," she said. "It's gross!"

"I didn't used to like it either," Marcia said haughtily, and I could just imagine her adding *when I was little*. "But now I do, and my parents let me have decaffeinated coffee once a week. With lots of milk."

"So what are you guys doing here?" I asked.

"Studying for our history test." Jessica pointed to a blue spiral notebook on the table next to them. I felt a nervous pang - with everything that was going on, I'd forgotten all about the history test we have next week! It's supposed to be HUGE, covering all the material we learned THE WHOLE year. Mrs. Santini said it was supposed to help us get used to the idea of final exams, like the kind we'll have in seventh grade. We're studying American history this year.

"Yeah, we borrowed Kellie's notes," Marcia added. I glanced over at the notebook, and what I saw made me knock over my mug of hot chocolate, spilling it all over the table.

"Oh my gosh, I'm so sorry!" I jumped up and started mopping up the hot chocolate with my napkin.

"You are such a klutz!" Marcia blurted out, as she stood up to avoid the cocoa that had begun dripping off the sides of the table.

"I'm really sorry," I apologized again. But as the waitress appeared to help us wipe up the mess, my mind was spinning. A piece of paper had been sticking out of the notebook, and it was covered in scribbles that perfectly matched the writing we had seen in the vault, with all those loops and hearts. *So that was why the handwriting had looked so familiar. It was Kellie's.* A cold feeling crept up my spine, and I tried to catch Sheila's eye, but she was busy collecting the wet napkins that were spread out all over the table.

How could I be so wrong about a person I thought was my friend?

****

My thoughts were interrupted by the ringing of a cell phone. Marcia fished around in her purse (what else!) and retrieved an iphone (again - what else?!).

"Oh hi!" she said after a pause. "Yeah, we're here at Greg's. I'll wait for you." She hung up. "That was my big sister," she explained, turning to Jessica. "She's here shopping for some clothes, and she said she'll pick us up here in about twenty minutes."

I reached over tremulously and picked up the blue notebook, trying to appear casual as I leafed through it. "Mind if I take a look at this?"

"Sure!" Marcia said. "But just give me that paper in the front." She held out her hand. "It's a letter I'm writing to my cousin in Italy, and it's private! We're going to visit her on our trip this summer," she added proudly.

I looked down at the notebook and pulled out the only piece of loose paper I saw. The one with the handwriting that resembled the future entry.

"Thanks." Marcia folded it up and put it in her purse. Just then, her phone rang again. "What is it, Jackie?" she said as she answered, sounding annoyed. "I told you we'd be here! We're right by the window!"

Relief coursed through my body as I realized what this meant.

Not Kellie. Not Kellie at all!

****

I got the check as fast as I could and practically pulled Sheila out of the restaurant. I was not going to sit with Marcia one minute longer than was absolutely necessary.

"So all we need now is a plan," I explained, as we rode home on our bikes. "Some way to sneak into Marcia's sister's room and search for the medallion when nobody's looking."

Easy-peasy, my foot.

By the time we reached my house, we had formulated a plan. Sheila would call Marcia and ask if we could come over and study with them, and somehow, while we were there, we'd figure out how to sneak into her sister's room and take the medallion. It could work, but it depended on so many things. Would Marcia let us come over? And would Jackie be home? If she was hanging out in her room, it would be impossible to go in. And what if she didn't even keep the medallion at her house?

When we came inside, my dad and RJ were sitting at the table playing Rat-a-tat-cat, which is RJ's favorite game these days. He won it at his friend's birthday party, and ever since then he's always bugging everybody to play it with him. I played a few times, but then I stopped because he ALWAYS CHEATS! The last time he did it, I got so mad, I threw my cards down on the table and stomped off to my room. He started crying like a little baby, and then of course *I* was the one who got in trouble. My mom sat down with me later and explained that RJ's too little to understand that cheating at games ruins them. Personally, I think that's ridiculous. I don't remember cheating at games when I was little!!

Sheila and I went out to the clubhouse and closed the door behind us.

"So, are you going to call now?" I flopped down on the red poof and put my head back. I was starting to get another headache.

"I guess." Sheila took her phone out of her backpack and looked up Marcia's number on the class Whatsapp group. She dialed slowly, and I could see her hands shaking.

"Hi Marcia!" Sheila said finally, with a cheerfulness I hoped Marcia couldn't tell was forced. "Um, Janie and I were wondering if we could come over and study with you guys this afternoon. We're really behind on the history stuff!"

I waited tensely until Sheila nodded her head and gave me a thumbs up. "Ok, great. We'll be over at one. Oh, yeah - thanks!" She hung up and grinned at me. "They're having pizza for lunch."

"Yay." I said, my voice flat. My stomach was doing flip flops, and to be honest, the thought of pizza made me kind of want to throw up.

The first part of our plan had been put into action. Now all we needed was a miracle.

****

When we got to Marcia's, it was nearly one-thirty. Marcia and Jessica were sitting around the kitchen table, surrounded by open pizza boxes, cans of juice and papers. They looked like they had actually been studying, which I found a bit hard to believe. Marcia isn't exactly *bookish*.

I looked around the kitchen. It was very modern and spotlessly clean. The kitchen table was black and shiny, and the walls were covered in wallpaper with tiny pink flowers on it.

"Have some pizza!" Marcia said, pushing one of the open boxes in my direction. My stomach did flip flops again as I caught a whiff of the burnt cheese and tomato sauce. I love pizza, but it really isn't something you want to be smelling when your stomach's upset.

"Um, no thanks," I said as Sheila accepted a large piece with onions and mushrooms. Sheila always likes toppings on her pizza. I know some people think it's babyish, but I can't stand anything but plain cheese. "I'm, uh, still full from the donuts and stuff at the mall."

"Suit yourself." Marcia helped herself to another piece and sat back down at the table. "We're still stuck on Chapter Eight," she said. Her mouth was full of pizza, and when she talked, you could see pieces of mushroom between her teeth. It was all *very* un-Marcia-like.

I studied her expression. She seemed very casual, very *unsuspicious*. Either we were completely wrong about her, or she was extremely confident we had no idea she had taken the medallion.

Jessica was holding the textbook in one hand and a cup of what looked like peach nectar in the other. "So, can I keep reading already?" she asked. "We don't have all day."

Marcia nodded, and as Jessica started reading, my mind wandered. I was definitely going to have to study when all of this was over. There was no way I could concentrate now. I watched the big hand on the round, over-sized clock that was hanging over the refrigerator. The minutes ticked by painfully slowly, and at two-thirty I stood up and pretended to stretch my legs.

"Where's the bathroom?" I asked, scanning Marcia's face for any sign she was on to me.

"Right down the hall." She pointed in the direction of the living room without even looking up.

"Ok, thanks." I reached out and quietly picked up Sheila's cell phone, putting a finger to my lips when she gave me a puzzled look. I slipped it into my pocket.

I crossed the living room, thinking again about how strangely *clean* everything was. It looked like real people didn't even live there.

My parents like to keep things relatively clean, and my mom can be a neat freak sometimes (even though I now know what a *slob* she was, when she was my age...) - but this was ridiculous. The sofa looked totally smooth, as if nobody ever sat on it. And the large Asian rug in the center of the room looked like it had just been vacuumed.

When I reached the bathroom, I opened and closed the door, so that anyone who was listening would think someone went inside. Then I turned to face the large staircase that led up to the second floor. I crossed my fingers and closed my eyes. *This had better work.* I didn't even want to think about the fact that we didn't have a backup plan.

I tiptoed up the stairs, cringing each time the floor creaked and pausing to make sure no one was coming. I was happy to see the stairs were covered in wall-to-wall carpeting, so my shoes didn't make any noise, but the creaking sounded to me like a herd of wild elephants. When I finally made it up the stairs, I stopped to catch my breath. I'm actually in pretty good shape, but I was so nervous, I must have been holding my breath or something.

I looked at the doors that led off the hallway, and my heart sank. There were at least six rooms up there! How would I be able to tell which one of them was Jackie's? And even if I did find it - what would I do if she was home?

I paused, straining to hear if there were sounds coming from any of the rooms, and relaxing just a little when I realized there weren't. That didn't mean anything, of course. If Jackie was sitting at her desk or playing on her computer or whatever, she could be completely silent.

I crept down the hall, peering through the open doors and mentally crossing each one off in my mind. The room with the huge double bed, white, shaggy wall-to-wall carpeting, freshly-painted walls and a dresser covered in perfume bottles was obviously her parents'. The next one, with a pink canopy bed and a huge Justin Bieber poster on the wall was definitely Marcia's. I was super curious - this was my chance to check out MTS's room!! - but I kept going anyway. On the other side of the hall were a study, a rec room and a door that led to a pristine bathroom. Which left -

At the very end of the hallway, I stopped in front of the only door that was closed. My heart was beating so hard, I was certain it could be heard a mile away, and I was sweating. I wiped my forehead with my sleeve and took several deep breaths. The door had a sign on it, made of wood with little acorns and leaves pasted on, and I gulped when I saw what it said:

Jackie's Room: Enter at your Own Risk!!

******

I stood outside the door, frantically going over my options in my mind. I could go back downstairs, rejoin the study group and pretend nothing was going on - but then we'd have to come back and try this whole thing again a different time. And the more time passed, the less likely we were to find the medallion. Who knew what Jackie would do with it? I didn't even know why she wanted it in the first place!

I put my ear up to the door, and I was dismayed to hear a low whirring noise from inside, like the sound of somebody operating some kind of a machine. This was crazy. I should just -

Before I realized what I was doing, I reached out and soundlessly pushed the door open. I breathed a sigh of relief when I saw what the whirring sound was - a hamster, or maybe a gerbil, running on a wheel. The room was dark, with just a computer screen glowing dimly in the far corner, on a desk that I was happy to see was unoccupied. The room was really messy and looked like it didn't even belong in this house.

My eyes were drawn to a small book that lay on the table next to the door: *"The Protectors of Fate"*. It had a cloth binding, like a diary, and had all kinds of pieces of paper sticking out of it. Without thinking, I grabbed it and put it in my pocket. I'm against stealing, but these were special circumstances! It was Jackie who had started the whole stealing thing, and I needed to find out what she was up to.

Then my heart stopped as my eyes adjusted to the dark. Jackie was asleep on her bed just two feet away from me, snoring softly and clutching the medallion – *my medallion!!!* - to her chest.

And it was then that I heard Marcia clambering up the stairs and shouting, "Janie? Are you up here?"

I stood frozen in place, afraid to breathe, and listened as Marcia went into room after room, calling out "Janie?" I could hear her hesitate outside Jackie's room, but I guess she took the sign on Jackie's door pretty seriously, because she soon turned and went back down the stairs, muttering, "That's strange."

I had come too far to just give up. So before my mind could tell me to walk away, my hand shot out and I carefully pried the medallion out of Jackie's grasp. I heard her turn over as I spun around and walked quickly out of the room.

Once downstairs, I slipped quietly outside and went around to knock on the back door that led into the kitchen.

"Janie, where were you?" Marcia said as she opened the door, a bewildered look on her face.

"Oh, sorry, I just went outside to call my mom." I handed the cell phone back to Sheila. "Actually, she said I need to come home now." I rolled my eyes and pretended to look annoyed. "My parents are going out and they need me to babysit RJ."

******

We rode back to my house as quickly as we could, and when we got inside, Sheila was surprised to see no one was home.

"Wait, so your mom didn't really need you to babysit?"

I chuckled, reaching into my pocket and pulling out the medallion. Sheila's eyes grew wide.

"How'd you get it back?" She exhaled sharply as the questions tumbled out. "Was Jackie home? Did you sneak into her room?"

I grinned at her, feeling relaxed for the first time in days. "Let's get some lemonade," I said, "and I'll tell you the whole story."

♥ May 14, 2011 ♥

Dear Diary,

Yup, it's still today. Actually, technically it might already be tomorrow. I always forget how that works. It's a bit after midnight, and we just got back from Kellie's Starbright Showdown!

It was INCREDIBLE!

After we got home from Marcia's, I filled Sheila in on everything that had happened, and I even showed her the strange book I took from Jackie's room. From now on, I'm keeping the medallion with me AT ALL TIMES, and for now I've found a really good hiding place for all the other stuff. I'm not writing where it is, in case someone finds this diary... I guess I'll have to buy a safe or something, if my parents let me.

I also checked the notes from Prof. Janie Ray, and I'm sure you won't be surprised to hear they were back to normal. What a relief! Being responsible for history going off track would be a bit much to handle.

At five, Sheila went home so that we could get dressed for the Showdown. I wore the new pink sweater and jeans I had worn to the movie group (well, new for me anyway - they came in the latest bag o'clothes from my cousins in Cleveland). And I put on a pair of heart-shaped gold earrings, even though they usually bother my ears.

We arrived at the studio at seven, just in time to meet up with Alexis and watch Kellie's pre-performance interview. She seemed nervous, but not as nervous as I would have been in her shoes! When she saw us, she gave us a big smile and motioned for us to come and sit down next to her.

"These are my best friends!" she said to the interviewer, and I managed a weak smile as the camera turned in our direction. I was definitely NOT expecting to be on TV! I looked at Sheila and was glad to see she also looked uncomfortable. Alexis had turned a distinct shade of green.

The performance was AMAZING, and as they announced the winners, Sheila and Alexis and I squeezed each other's hands tightly. Kellie ended up winning second place! Which meant she would get free voice lessons for a year, and probably even the chance to make her own album!

The rest of the evening was a blur. We managed to congratulate Kellie after the show, but she was surrounded by so many people, we couldn't really talk. Before we left, I gave her a big hug.

"You're a great friend, Kellie," I said, vowing to never doubt her again.

"So are you, Janie," she answered warmly. A happy glow settled over me.

****

Now that we've found the medallion and everything's back to normal (or, at least, as normal as it can be these days), I'm REALLY freaking out about my history test!! I can't believe I haven't studied yet. Even *Marcia's* been working on it for days already.

And in the next few days, I'll have to take a look at Jackie's book - the one about The Protectors of Fate. I wonder what that's all about!

My mind keeps going back to Grandpa Charlie's warning in the very first note he gave us, when we visited him in 1985: *Everything is going to change.*

He sure was right about that!

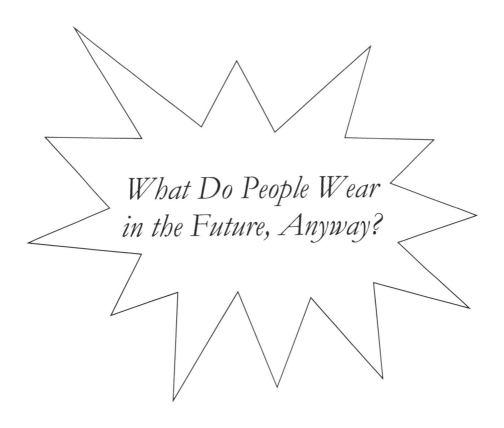

What Do People Wear in the Future, Anyway?

♥ May 18, 2011 ♥

Dear Diary,

Today we had that big history test I told you about. It was *really* hard, but I think I did pretty well. And there's at least one question I aced for sure:

Who was Penelope Barker and what was her contribution to the American Revolution?

LOL. I think I got *that* one right. I left out the part about her having a really cool way of climbing into her bedroom window, though.

The past few days at school have been, er, pretty awkward. I have no idea what to do about Marcia! She's still acting all buddy-buddy, like nothing's wrong, and Alexis and Kellie have no clue what she did. They don't know about the medallion of course, and I'm not allowed to tell them anything. So when Marcia asks to sit with us and stuff, we can't exactly tell her where to go, because Alexis and Kellie wouldn't understand why.

Like today at lunch.

It was make-your-own-taco day – which everybody *loves*, because the stuff is actually *good*. I don't know why, but tacos seem to be the one thing the school cafeteria can pull off pretty well. I used to think tacos were gross, but then one day last summer my mom made this whole project of making them from scratch, and since then I've liked them. We watched a YouTube video on how to make the dough and roll it out and everything, and we made our own meat sauce. YUM!!

I took three tacos, loaded them up with meat, lettuce, cheese and salsa, and Sheila, Alexis and Kellie and I headed for a table in the corner to talk about Kellie's (incredible!!!) Starbright victory. She's acting like nothing special happened, but winning second place is actually a HUGE deal. She gets a full college scholarship and a cash prize of $100,000 (!!!). Her parents are letting her use $500 to buy whatever she wants, and making her put the rest into a savings plan for when she's older. And she gets to make her very own album, which will be for sale all over the country!!

"Ew, this table's dirty," Alexis said, wrinkling her nose and waving her hand in front of her face. "And it smells. Isn't there someplace else we can sit?"

We looked around the room, but all the other tables were taken. The cafeteria tends to get crowded on taco day.

"Here, hold this." Sheila gave Alexis her tray, rummaged around in her backpack and pulled out one of those disposable wet wipes you get at restaurants and places like that. When she saw us looking at her, she flushed and shrugged her shoulders. "What? We went to Carlos' Pizza last night, and I kept a couple as souvenirs."

Kellie giggled. "You took a souvenir from *Carlos' Pizza*? Gee, you don't get out much, do you?"

I snickered. Sheila always keeps stuff like that, and her room is full of things she refuses to throw out – like bus tickets from all of her vacations and movie tickets from special occasions. She even still has her ticket from that time we saw Never Say Never with Calvin and that whole gang! She calls it her "first date with Calvin", even though it *obviously* doesn't count.

Sheila snorted and wiped the table, ignoring us. Then, as we sat down and started eating, I remembered the one thing I *don't* like about tacos. They're kind of hard to eat without making a mess. And let's just say I'm not exactly the *neatest* person in the world.

I opened up my tacos and started spooning the contents carefully out onto a plate. I wasn't taking any chances, especially with the brand new turquoise sweater I was wearing. I figured if I ate the meat and vegetables with a fork, I could eat the empty tacos last and avoid spraying sauce all over my clothes.

Alexis raised an eyebrow at me. "Janie, what are you doing?"

"I'm, uh -"

"Oh, that's a good idea!" Kellie interjected, emptying her own tacos onto a plate. She looked at Alexis. "See, that way we won't make a huge mess!"

"Oh, cool. I mean, it looks kind of awful, but I guess it's better to eat it than to wear it!"

We all giggled. "So Kellie," I said, taking a bite of the meat and vegetable mixture. It *did* look kind of disgusting, now that I thought about it. I looked away – I was *starving*, and I wasn't about to ruin my appetite by grossing myself out. "How does it feel to be an actual star? It must be so amazing!!"

"I guess…" Kellie answered. "I mean, I'm really happy I won and everything, and I'm totally psyched to make my own album. But some other weird stuff has been happening, and I'm not sure how I feel about it."

I frowned. "What do you mean?"

"Well, for one thing, our phone has been practically ringing off the hook since Saturday night. My parents are going to have to change the number and make sure it stays private. And I've started getting fan mail. Yesterday, the mailman brought us a whole *sack* of letters from people all around the country! I started reading them last night, and some of them are really sweet. My mom wants me to read as many as I can— she says if someone's gone to the trouble to write to me, I should try and answer them. I guess she's right, but now I have to spend a whole hour doing that every day!"

"Wow!" Sheila said, her eyes wide. "I still can't believe it. You're like a real live celebrity!"

Kellie shook her head. "Don't get carried away. I'm sure all the attention will die down after a few days. But the other crazy thing is -" She hesitated.

"What?" Sheila said impatiently.

"Well… It's just that American Girl magazine wants to interview me next week."

Sheila choked on her taco, and Alexis started coughing like crazy, water coming out of her nose. Luckily, I didn't have anything in my mouth, but my eyes practically bugged out of my head. We all stared at her wordlessly for several moments, our mouths open.

"Holy Macaroni," Sheila finally said.

I poked her. "That doesn't even rhyme, banana brain."

She rolled her eyes. "Kellie just told us that she's about to become completely famous, and *that's* all you can think about?"

Kellie looked nervous. "I guess I'm excited about it, but to be honest, I'm terrified. Just because I can sing well doesn't mean I can talk in an *interview*. Somehow, when I'm on stage, my music helps me forget how terrified I am. But talking about myself is a completely different thing. What if I say something completely embarrassing? And what if everyone who reads the interview thinks I'm the dorkiest person in the world? And the worst part is -" She stopped and took a long drink of water.

"What?" Sheila asked again.

Kellie had picked up her napkin and was twisting it around anxiously. "They kind of said they want to put my picture on the cover."

I guess that was as much as Sheila could take, because she jumped up and started shrieking like a crazy person, giving Kellie a huge hug. "That is the awesomest thing *ever*!!" she said.

Kellie hugged her back. "Thanks, Sheila. I don't know. I'm really,

really glad I won and stuff, but I kind of just want to go back to my regular life."

"Yeah, I would be completely bummed if I suddenly became really rich and famous," Sheila said with a smirk.

"I know," I said, shaking my head sadly. "Some people are just so unlucky."

Kellie grinned. "Yeah, I guess I shouldn't knock it. And I am happy about it. Really."

I reached into my pocket and fingered the medallion, smiling to myself and trying to absorb everything that Kellie had said. If it hadn't been for the medallion, none of this would have happened, and Kellie would probably still be Sardine Girl. I shook my head and shuddered. The whole thing was preposterous. And yet - it was true.

Out of the corner of my eye, I could see Marcia approaching our table. She was wearing a bright orange miniskirt, a dark brown v-neck top and sandals, and - as usual - her hair was flawless.

I elbowed Sheila and cast a meaningful glance in Marcia's direction. Sheila shrugged as if to say, "Don't ask me." I sighed. This was *definitely* going to be weird.

"Hi guys!" Marcia said cheerfully, sliding into a chair across from Kellie. She unfolded her napkin and put it in her lap.

I eyed her suspiciously. How could she act like nothing had happened?

"Hi!" Alexis said with a friendly smile. The great thing about Alexis is that she's nice to pretty much everybody. She's a very uncomplicated person, and she usually assumes the best about people. Even Marcia. It's been really important to her that we give Marcia a chance, and she's convinced that if we're just nice to her, Marcia will stop being such a jerk.

If only.

"Um, hi Marcia!" I managed.

But Marcia's attention was already focused on Kellie.

Of course.

"So, Kellie," Marcia was saying, taking a dainty bite of her taco. It would so *figure* Marcia could eat tacos without spilling anything. "You must be really excited about Starbright! What was it like?"

Kellie smiled politely. "Yeah, I'm pretty excited. I still can't really believe it's all happening, you know?"

"Yeah, I know." Marcia gave Kellie a knowing look. "I have a cousin who had a part in a movie once, and people who had always ignored him started acting like they were his best friends. Well don't worry – if people start bothering you, we'll tell them where to get off. I mean, we're your *real* friends."

Sheila snorted, and I elbowed her again. Marcia was nothing if not *oblivious*.

"Oh Marcia," Alexis said suddenly, reaching into her backpack. "I forgot to give you an invitation to my Couch Potato Party."

The end of the year Couch Potato Party has sort of become a tradition for me and Sheila, and this year Alexis decided to host one. It's basically a sleep over party on the last day of school (or a few days later), where we bake, watch movies and eat tons of junk food. We've been doing it since second grade, and it's really fun. If Marcia ends up coming, it will kind of ruin it for me, but I can't think of any good reason Alexis shouldn't invite her – or, at least, not any good reason I can tell Alexis about...

Marcia ignored Alexis and continued peppering Kellie with questions. "So, are you getting tons of fan mail and stuff? Are people asking for your autograph?"

There was an uncomfortable silence, as Kellie looked from Alexis to Marcia. "Um, Marcia, I think Alexis was trying to give you something."

"What? Oh, sorry." Marcia turned to Alexis and offered her a sweet smile. She took the invitation and looked at it. "What is this?"

Alexis sighed. "It's an invitation to my Couch Potato Party. It's a sleepover I'm having on the last day of school. We're gonna just veg out in front of the TV, eat junk food and stuff like that."

"Oh, cool." Marcia folded the invitation and stuffed it into the pocket of her miniskirt. "I think I'll be able to come." She smiled again before turning back to Kellie.

"So, I was thinking. My big sister sells a lot of stuff on eBay, and I was wondering if you could give us some autographed things of yours. I'll bet we could get a huge amount of money for some clothes and stuff signed by you. What do you say? And *of course* we'd give you some of the money." She waited hopefully.

At the mention of Marcia's big sister, I froze in my seat, swallowing hard. *Jackie! The reason why Marcia had stolen my medallion in the first place!*

I glanced over at Sheila and shook my head helplessly. It was so *bizarre* how Marcia was acting like nothing had happened, and even mentioning her big sister like it was the most natural thing in the world!

Kellie rolled her eyes. "Sorry, Marcia, I'm not really into that idea. But thanks anyway."

Marcia looked disappointed. Finally, after finishing her second taco, she stood up and picked up her tray. "Well guys, I guess I'll see you later. Toodeloo!" she sang and waved her fingers at us.

As she walked away, Sheila and I took deep breaths and sighed at the same time.

"Jinx, buy me a coke!" I said automatically.

"You can't do that for a *sigh*," Sheila said indignantly.

"Why not? Is it against the Jinx Buy Me A Coke Manual?" I giggled.

Sheila just grunted in reply.

"So, what are you planning to do with your $500?" Alexis asked Kellie. Her voice was strained, and I had the feeling she was trying to change the subject so we wouldn't have to talk about Marcia.

Kellie's face lit up. "Well, for starters I'm going to buy a ridiculous amount of music and a ukulele." The ukulele was the newest instrument Kellie was into, and she had been talking for weeks about getting a handmade one. "And I'm, uh, taking my parents out for a fancy dinner in a few days."

Sheila and Alexis exchanged glances and then looked away from each other, and I could have sworn things suddenly got awkward. I gave Sheila a questioning look, but she avoided my eyes. Or at least I think she did.

What the heck...?

Then the bell rang and we all grabbed our trays and headed for fifth period. I sighed. It was only one o'clock, and I was already ready to crawl back into bed and hide under the covers.

******

After school, Sheila came over so that we could take a look at the strange book I had taken from Marcia's sister Jackie's room – the one that had *"Protectors of Fate"* on the front cover.

Just so you know, I'm not usually a thief. I think stealing is W-R-O-N-G, and normally I would never take *anything* that didn't belong to me. Once, when I was like five, I opened the drawer of the end table on my dad's side of the bed and found a bunch of change – quarters, dimes, nickels and pennies. It was probably all of two dollars, but it seemed like a lot to me. I was still at the age when I thought five pennies were more than one quarter, because five is more than one and all that. I didn't really understand the concept of money.

Anyway, I got really excited, because I had just gotten a new piggy bank, and I needed something to put in it – so I took the coins and hid them in my room. I didn't mean to do anything wrong, but when my parents found out, they sat me down and we had this whole long talk about stealing and taking things that belong to other people. They didn't exactly get mad, but I remember crying a lot. I guess I felt really guilty. Maybe I was afraid I'd end up like one of those bad guys on TV or something!

So you get the idea. I'm not exactly the kind of person who goes into people's rooms and takes their stuff. But the business with Jackie's book is a special situation.

Anyway, when we got to my house after school, the door was locked and it looked like nobody was home. I fished around in the huge flowerpot on our front porch, and sure enough – the key was there.

"I guess my mom's not home. Cool, we'll have the house to ourselves." I unlocked the door and pushed it open, quickly turning on the light in the front hallway. I really, really don't like dark houses. They creep me out.

We headed straight for the kitchen, dumping our bags on the table and practically collapsing into the big, wooden chairs we got last year from the neighborhood yard sale. My parents are big believers in used furniture, and they get most of it on the internet. My dad says it's better for the environment, because making new stuff uses up a lot of natural resources. Plus, you can get much better things for less money.

"You hungry?" I asked Sheila.

She shook her head and rubbed her tummy. "Nah. Still full from lunch. Let's just grab some cookies."

I opened the freezer and took out a big container of homemade gluten free chocolate-chip cookies. You probably remember that RJ is gluten free. A lot of gluten free stuff is gross, but the chocolate-chip cookies my mom makes are AMAZING! Especially when they're frozen. And who said you have to be hungry to eat cookies?

"Here, put these on a plate," I said, handing the container to Sheila. "I'll be right back." I ran upstairs to my room, grabbed Jackie's book from under my mattress, and we headed out to the clubhouse.

"Don't forget the cookies," I called out to Sheila over my shoulder.

"Me? Forget cookies?" Sheila grinned. "Not likely."

******

As we settled down on the floor of the clubhouse, I held up the book and turned it around in my hands. It was small and green, with a cloth binding, and it actually looked a bit like a diary. I opened it carefully, trying to keep all the little pieces of paper that were stuck inside from falling out, and turned to the first page. I cleared my throat and started to read aloud.

*****

"Janie! Where are you? It's dinner time!" I heard my mom calling from inside the house. I put the book down and rubbed my eyes, standing up and stretching.

"What time is it?" I asked Sheila.

She rubbed her eyes too. "I don't know," she replied, pulling her phone out of her back pocket. "Whoa! It's seven-thirty! We've been reading for *hours*."

"Wow," I said. I took off my scrunchie and redid my ponytail, blinking to refocus my eyes. "Pretty incredible stuff, too."

"Yeah," Sheila said. "We're in seriously deep doo-doo."

"I guess that's one way of putting it," I exhaled slowly.

******

Sheila went home shortly after that, and I came inside for dinner. My mom and RJ had already set the table, and my dad was just getting home from work.

I think I may have told you that my dad's an electrician. My mom's a writer, and she works from home. She writes lots of interesting stuff, and even some kids' books sometimes. But I don't usually read her books, because it feels kind of weird – especially when she uses stuff from our life for her stories!

Like once she wrote this really funny book about a little brother and big sister who are always fighting. She made the little brother gluten free, and the big sister was always complaining about her frizzy hair! Even some of their fights sounded eerily familiar – and I found myself cringing every time I turned the page and saw something else that reminded me of our family. She swore she didn't really base them on us, but let's just say I remain unconvinced.

"Hi, Muffin," my dad said, patting me on the head as he hung up his jacket.

"Hi, Daddy!" I said, giving him a hug. I love the way my dad smells – like outside – raked leaves and fresh air - and like *safety*. There's just something about him that always makes me feel like everything's going to be ok. And generally, he's a really good problem solver. But this time I didn't think he'd be able to help me.

"Oh, hi Mark!" My mom said, coming over and giving my dad a kiss. "You made it just in time. Dinner's on the table."

Both my parents know how to cook, and my dad always says it's not the 1950's anymore (whatever *that* means). When I was little, he stayed home with me for a couple of years while my mom worked out of the house, and he always does the laundry. Now that Mom's working from home, she ends up doing most of the cooking and stuff. But she makes a big point of telling me that if she worked in an office like Dad does, they'd split the housework fifty-fifty.

She says that past generations of women worked very hard to make things equal, and she doesn't want me to get the wrong idea. But I don't see what she's getting so worked up about. It's totally obvious that women can do whatever they want – I mean, geez, there are even women running for president! The other day, when we were in the car on the way home from school, RJ suddenly asked whether boys can be doctors too. Just like that, right out of the blue! My mom started cracking up and laughed so hard coffee actually came out of her nose! Later I heard her telling my dad about it, and he laughed too and said that here was the proof that feminism had won. Honestly, I have no idea what he was talking about. I figure RJ just thought only girls could be doctors, since our pediatrician, Dr. Smith, is a woman.

We sat down at the table, and even before I could pick up my fork, my mom launched into our usual dinner conversation - where everyone tells about the best and worst things that happened to them during the day. We've been doing that since I was little - my parents say that since we're all so busy during the day, it's really important to have dinner together and talk about stuff. Luckily, RJ was dying to tell them about a kid who grabbed the ball from him during recess, because my mind was just one big jumble, full of all the weird stuff we had read about in Jackie's book.

It turns out that the Protectors of Fate is a secret society, kind of like a club, that Jackie belongs to at her college. According to the book, there are branches of the society at lots of different schools, and each branch has just about twelve members. Each year, three freshmen get a secret invitation to join, and they're not allowed to tell *anyone* about it. The society has been around for hundreds of years, and even when people leave college they are supposed to keep in touch with other members. And if they stay loyal to the society, they get all kinds of crazy things, like a new car on the day of graduation and the money to buy a really nice house when they turn thirty.

So far so creepy. But that's just the tip of the iceberg. Turns out the *whole entire purpose* of the Protectors of Fate is to make it so that the Bearer of the Medallion can't do their job. From the book it seems like they don't know exactly what the medallion is, or what it can do. They just know that they're supposed to do whatever it takes to prevent it from being used to avert disasters. They work for a small group of people who call themselves *The Privileged*. People who actually think it's their *job* to rule over all of humanity. And they figure if there are lots of catastrophes, they'll be able to use them to gain control over people. Like the Pharaohs in Egypt.

A shiver went down my spine as I remembered some of the other people the book said had been Bearers of the Medallion throughout history. Einstein. Thomas Jefferson. People who had changed the path of humanity! I thought back to the strange quote we saw on the wall of the bank the first time we visited the vault with the secret histories. *"The only reason for time is so that everything doesn't happen at once – Albert Einstein"*. I shivered again. If Albert Einstein was a Bearer of the Medallion, that quote suddenly made a whole lot more sense.

"Janie?" I looked up to see my parents and RJ eyeing me expectantly.

"Huh?"

My mom shook her head and gave Dad one of her *"tweens, what can you do?"* looks. "It's your turn, Janie. And you haven't even touched your food."

I glanced down at my plate and realized that I hadn't taken even one bite since the beginning of dinner. I grinned sheepishly and shrugged my shoulders. "Sorry, I guess I'm just a bit distracted."

"You think? Anything you want to tell us about, honey?" My mom looked concerned.

I shrugged again. "No, no big deal."

"So we're waiting to hear. What's the best thing that happened to you today?"

"Uh…" I tried desperately to remember what had happened at school that morning. Finally I said, "I guess the history test. It was pretty easy. And Kellie! She's being interviewed by American Girl next week. And they want to put her on the cover!"

"Wow!" my mom sat back in her chair, looking impressed. "That's great! Her parents must be very proud of her."

I nodded. I don't think my parents have any idea that I was the one who got Kellie on Starbright in the first place. I mean, they know Kellie slept over that night, but other than that – no clue.

"And what was the worst thing that happened?" My dad prompted me to continue.

"Well..." I couldn't very well tell them about the weirdness of seeing Marcia in school. And I *definitely* couldn't tell them about the book Sheila and I had been reading all afternoon. "Um, I can't really think of anything."

"That's great!" my dad said, grinning. "Imagine that – a perfect day at school."

I grinned back at him. "Hey, that doesn't mean I like school." I said. "I wouldn't want you to get the wrong idea or anything."

After I helped clear the table and load the dishwasher, I ran upstairs to my room and closed the door, flopping down on my bed and picking up Jackie's book.

I put it under my pillow and closed my eyes, thoughts whirling around in my head. The truly strange thing about the book was how the Protectors of Fate really seemed to believe that they were the good guys and that it was the *Bearers of the Medallion* who were messing up history. They really thought everyone would be better off if the Privileged *did* control everything, since they were destined to rule and knew best how to keep order. They actually saw democracy as a kind of unsafe chaos, where nobody was really in charge and lots of bad things could happen. And they thought it was their job to keep the medallion *safe* from the Bearer, so that history could take its natural course.

My eyelids started feeling heavy and I closed them, figuring I'd just rest for a few minutes before getting up to do my homework.

And just before I dropped into what ended up being a very long and very deep sleep, I was struck by a horrifying realization that made my hair stand on end.

The Protectors of Fate existed solely to prevent me from being Bearer of the Medallion. And they would do whatever *it took to achieve their goal.*

♥ May 19, 2011 ♥

Dear Diary,

I woke with a start and sat up abruptly, my heart pounding. Rubbing my eyes, I picked up my alarm clock and peered bleary-eyed at the screen. It was only 6:00. I had another twenty minutes until I had to get up.

I sighed and sank back down on my pillow, closing my eyes and taking several deep breaths to calm myself down. This whole thing was getting *really* out of hand. And I had literally *no* idea what I was going to do about it.

Plus, I had fallen asleep without doing my math homework. URGH!! I'm pretty sure I've mentioned I HATE math, right??

I groaned and pulled myself up again, squinting as I headed for the bathroom. Somehow, when I had been with Sheila yesterday, I hadn't realized the full implications of what we were reading. It was only later that the true meaning of Jackie's book had sunken in.

Deep doo-doo, indeed.

I quickly brushed my teeth and pulled on some clothes, barely noticing what I grabbed from the closet. As you know, I'm not exactly the most fashion-conscious person in the world. But this morning I outdid even myself, putting on plaid pants and a striped shirt. It was only after I sat down at the kitchen table and noticed my mom looking at me funny, that I realized what I was wearing. I groaned again and went back upstairs to change. Which of course meant I ended up having to run out of the house without doing my math homework.

It was barely 7:30, and this was already shaping up to be a truly amazing day.

******

As soon as I got to school I went looking for Sheila, and rolled my eyes when I saw her – once again – talking to Calvin in the hallway next to her locker. She was so engrossed in the conversation with him that she didn't even see me coming. I stood there with my arms crossed, tapping my foot and waiting for her to notice me.

It was Calvin who finally looked up. "Hi, Janie!" he said with a friendly grin. He was wearing ripped jeans and a button down shirt, his wavy blond hair combed to the side. He really was very cute, and I could almost see why Sheila liked him so much. Although I still didn't understand why she made such a big deal about boys.

Sheila turned around, surprised. "Oh, hi Janie!" She reached out and touched my arm, smiling. "I'm sorry, I didn't see you there."

I rolled my eyes again. "It's ok," I said. "I just need to talk to you a minute, ok?"

She gave me a puzzled look. Could she have forgotten everything we read yesterday? Or did she just not realize its significance?

I pulled Sheila into the bathroom (in case you haven't noticed, that's where most of our important conversations happen, at least in school) and checked to make sure nobody else was inside. "We need to talk," I said in a low voice.

"Um, ok." Sheila turned to face me. "You mean about what we read yesterday?"

"Of course about what we read yesterday!" I was starting to get annoyed. Why was Sheila acting like this was no big deal?? "You realize what this means, don't you?"

Sheila just looked at me. Finally she said, "Yeah. I mean, I think I do."

"Well then, you get that we are in a lot of danger! Jackie and her friends will do anything to get their hands on the medallion!"

Sheila nodded her head, suddenly serious. "Yeah. So what do you think we should do?"

"That's just it. I have no idea! I don't even know where to start!" I was horrified to realize that tears were welling up in my eyes, and I studied my fingernails carefully to avoid looking at Sheila.

"Hey Janie," Sheila said softly, reaching out and squeezing my shoulder. "It's gonna be ok, I'm sure of it! We'll figure out what to do, just like we did when the medallion went missing. Remember what your Grandpa Charlie said?"

"What, you mean that everything would change?" I reached up and brushed a tear off my face.

"Yeah, but also that you'd be able to handle it. Come on, the bell's about to ring. Let's just hold tight for a bit and we'll figure something out."

I sniffed and walked over to the sink to wash my face. The last thing I needed was for people to see me crying, on top of everything else. I gave Sheila a grateful smile.

Boy, was I glad we were in this together.

******

The rest of the day dragged by, and I tried to put the whole thing out of my mind and concentrate on school. MUCH easier said than done. Finally the last bell rang and I grabbed my backpack and ran outside.

And it was while I was unlocking my bike and putting my helmet on that I first noticed the strange girl, standing by the bus lane and looking very lost.

She was wearing really odd clothes – dark navy pants that looked like spandex leggings with weird, bell-bottom cuffs and what I can only describe as an orange tunic. She had long frizzy hair – kind of like mine, come to think of it – and these big brown glasses with the thickest lenses I've ever seen. Her hair, which was bright silver and looked like it had been spray-painted, flew wildly in every direction. Every so often she reached up and pushed it out of her eyes. She was holding a large brown bag - kind of like a purse, but really ugly - and a small, rectangular device that looked like tablet. She seemed to be about our age, and I watched as she walked back and forth and muttered to herself.

I was so mesmerized by her strange appearance that I didn't notice Sheila come up behind me, and I nearly jumped two feet in the air when she tapped me on the shoulder.

"Who's distracted now?" she asked wryly, raising her right eyebrow. I love Sheila's eyebrows – they're very expressive.

I poked her and pointed at the girl. "Who's that?" I asked, trying to be discreet.

"Who is what?" Sheila looked up and her face took on a look of surprise when she saw the girl. "Wow, I don't know. I don't think I've seen her before."

The girl must have seen us pointing and staring, because she started walking in our direction.

"Uh oh," I said, bending over and pretending to be really busy inspecting the gears on my bike. "It looks like she's coming over here."

Sheila – being, as she is, Sheila – smiled broadly and waved in the girl's direction. "Hi!" she said, sticking her hand out as the girl approached us. "My name is Sheila. What's yours?"

I swallowed and stood up, kind of wishing I could disappear into thin air. I love that Sheila's a very friendly person, but sometimes she takes it a bit – *far*.

The girl just stood there, quietly appraising us. She didn't even smile or take Sheila's hand, and for a while we all stood there stiffly.

"Um, so where are you from?" Sheila managed after a few seconds. Leave it to her to break the awkward silence.

The girl still didn't say anything, though. She was staring at me, and seemed to be pointing her little device at my face.

Then she said, "You're Janie Ray."

I barely managed a small nod.

"Good!" she said briskly. Then she pointed the device at Sheila and for just a moment, her mouth dropped open. She recovered quickly, though, and for the first time offered us a small grin. "And you're Sheila. My name is Sheila too, by the way. Sheila Ray. I was named after my great-grandmother," she added matter-of-factly. "People call me Lia, though. That's my nickname."

"Oh, cool." Sheila said, grinning back.

Meanwhile, my mind was spinning. Sheila Ray? *My mom is Sheila Ray.* Was the girl some kind of a relative? I was pretty sure I knew all my relatives, even my second cousins, and I certainly didn't think I had any family members that were so – bizarre. I tried to remember what my mom had told me about her name. Was she named after some old ancestor?

I met Sheila's eyes, and before I could say anything, the girl continued, "This is 2011, right?" She looked around. "Wow. It's not anything like the history books."

Then it hit me with the force of a punch in the stomach, and I nearly dropped my bike and fell over. *If her great-grandmother's name was Sheila...*

I gulped and grabbed onto the bike, steadying myself as the implications of my realization sunk in. She was from the future, and probably a Bearer of the Medallion. The medallion, I knew, was passed down from grandparent to grandchild, like I had gotten it from Grandpa Charlie.

My thoughts were interrupted by the girl, who had thrown her arms around me. "Grandma!" she exclaimed with a wide smile, snuggling up to me. "It's so good to see you!"

******

I must have blacked out, because the next thing I knew, I was sprawled out on my back in the clubhouse with my feet up on a stack of books. Sheila was hovering over me, fanning me with a folded-up piece of paper, and the girl was sitting on the big, red poof, playing with her little device.

I sat up quickly and held onto Sheila's arm, feeling dizzy. "What happened?"

"You fainted." Sheila put her hand on my forehead. "Are you ok?" Her voice was concerned.

"I – I think so." I pushed myself up and stood, wobbling just a bit on my feet. "H – how'd we get back here? Weren't we at school?"

Sheila wrinkled her nose and gestured toward the other Sheila. Er, Lia. "She did it. I don't know how. One minute we were in the bus lane, and the next…" Her voice trailed off.

My eyes widened and I stared at the girl, who brushed off our amazement with a flick of her hand.

"What, you've never seen a Teleporter before?" she asked disdainfully. When we didn't answer she sighed. "Ok, yeah – I remember reading that the Teleporter was only invented in the 5o's. Sorry. I know you guys still use cars and stuff." She shook her head woefully. "I keep forgetting how old fashioned you are."

Sheila looked offended. "Old fashioned?!" She pulled her cell out of her pocket and shoved it in the other Sheila's face. "You call this old fashioned?"

"Wow!" the girl said, taking the phone and turning it over in her hands. "An antique phone!" Her voice was awed and she didn't seem to be teasing.

Which, of course, only made Sheila madder. "Antique?!" she huffed, folding her arms across her chest.

The girl and I exchanged a grin. Sheila could be pretty funny.

Then a chill went down my back, as I remembered who she was. *My granddaughter.* I shivered as I studied her more closely, taking in her strange outfit and glasses. She would have been pretty if she hadn't been wearing such weird clothes and if her hair weren't so wild. I wondered vaguely if her mom was also always trying to get her to put her hair in a ponytail. Then I caught myself. *Her mom.* Would that be... *my daughter?* Or was I her grandmother on her father's side?

The girl – Lia - turned to me. "Yeah, your mom." Then she faced Sheila. "I'm sorry, I didn't mean to insult you. It's just -" She cleared her throat. "Nobody's used a *phone* in at least twenty years."

My eyes widened and I stared at her, unable to process what had just happened. *Lia had read my mind!!!* Was she a psychic or something? Then I flushed as I remembered the unflattering things I had been thinking about her clothes and hair. I sure hoped she didn't read *those* thoughts! I glanced at her out of the corner of my eye and she gave me a slight nod, holding her hair back as if to put it in a ponytail and grinning.

O.M.G. I flushed again and looked down at the floor.

"So what do you use if not phones?" Sheila was asking. "Texting? Email?"

Lia chuckled softly. "Email? Wow. No, silly. We use apps."

"Oh, apps! We have apps too!" Sheila said excitedly. "What kinds of apps?"

"Well, there's the Teleporter, which you saw. The Identifier..."

"The Identifier? What's that?"

The girl looked surprised. "You don't have that, either? Well, it's just something that identifies you by reading your DNA."

"Your what?" Sheila asked.

"Your DNA. You know, your genes."

We must have looked confused, because she kept on explaining. "Each person has their own unique genetic code that they get from their parents. In the olden days, you used to need an actual sample from a person to read it – like a piece of hair or some blood or something."

"Oh, like on those TV shows!" I said. "Like when they take someone's DNA to solve a crime."

The girl just kind of looked at me, but I could see Sheila nodding.

"Anyway, these days – or rather, in my time - we can read a person's DNA just by scanning a picture of them. And then we can find out all kind of things about them – like who they are, who they are related to, and stuff like that. Everybody's DNA is in this huge database."

"But wait," Sheila said. "How were you able to identify us? *We* aren't even from your time!"

I elbowed her. "We aren't from her time *now*, doodlebrain. But our older selves are, and a person's DNA doesn't change."

Sheila looked sheepish. "Right. Ok, so what other apps do you have?"

The girl looked down at the floor and then back up at us, her face suddenly serious. "Well, that's partly why I came looking for you. Things have gotten completely out of control, and I desperately need your help!"

******

Five minutes later, we were sitting together on the floor of the clubhouse, sipping tall glasses of lemonade and listening to Lia tell her story.

"In my time it's the year 2071. Things started getting really bad about twenty years ago, before I was born, when The Privileged managed to take control."

I coughed and just barely managed to avoid spitting out my lemonade as the blood drained from my face. "They took control? How?" Then it hit me. Twenty years ago, before Lia was born, I was Bearer of the Medallion.

The Privileged had taken control on my watch.

"That's the thing," she continued. "We don't really *know* how. What we do know is that twenty-five years ago, the medallion stopped working. This was the first time I've ever been able to use it."

"You mean, this is your first trip through time?" Sheila interrupted.

"Yup." The girl nodded.

"So what happened?" I asked. "Did the Protectors of Fate get their hands on it? Did they do something to it?"

She nodded again. "They developed a device that somehow prevents the medallion from working. They were smart – they didn't *steal* the medallion again, because they knew we would eventually find it and get it back. Instead, they used some new technology to drain it of its magic. We don't know how it works. You've spent the past twenty years of your life trying to figure it out!"

"So how did you get here?" Sheila asked.

The girl lowered her voice. "About a year ago, you found something in one of the Histories. Luckily, the Privileged never found out about the Vault and were never able to take those away." She reached into her pocket and pulled out a familiar silver and black key with the number 451 imprinted on it in big white letters. "See, I've still got the key."

Sheila's eyes widened. "Is the bank still there in your time? Is Michael still-"

Lia shook her head. "No, unfortunately Michael passed away. His son has replaced him in the Outer Circle."

The Outer Circle – kind of like the good-guys equivalent of the Protectors of Fate. People who vaguely knew of the medallion's existence, and helped the Bearer in all kinds of ways, but didn't know exactly what it was capable of.

"Go on," I urged impatiently. "What did she find in the

Histories?"

Sheila snorted. "You mean, what did *you* find in the Histories."

I couldn't repress a small smile. "Right."

"Well, it turns out that the Ancient Greek philosophers, even though they lived such a long time ago, understood more about the universe than we give them credit for. One of the earliest ones, a guy named Thales, discovered the secret to reading minds! He laid it all out in a treatise that has remained hidden in the vault for centuries, like a needle in a haystack. You spent decades reading all those Histories, trying desperately to find something that could help us against the Privileged, and finally came across it last year."

She paused and took a long drink of her lemonade, while I waited for her to continue, chewing nervously on my fingernails.

"You already know that in the future you become a professor, right?" she asked. I nodded. "Well, you're actually a physicist. And, with the help of another scientist in the Outer Circle, you managed to take Thales' discoveries and turn them into this." She pulled out her device and tapped on the screen a couple of times before giving it to me.

I took her device, my hands trembling, and looked at the screen. *The Mindreader.* An app that made it so you could read other people's thoughts! Sheila leaned over my shoulder and we stared at it blankly for a few seconds before handing it back to her.

So that was how she had read my mind earlier!

Before I could say anything, Sheila snorted. ""Hold on a second. Janie *hates* math. It's her worst subject! And you expect us to believe she became a *physicist?* That's -" she paused. "That's *insane!*"

I burst out laughing. We were dealing with apps that could teleport people and read people's minds, and I was being visited by my *future granddaughter*. But Sheila was busy getting all worked up about the fact that I ended up becoming a physicist. Then again, she did have a point. Me and math?? Never!

The girl eyed me strangely and then said, "You hate math? That's interesting. I do too! But you're the one who always tells me how important it is and can't seem to understand why I don't like it!"

I frowned. "I always tell myself that when I grow up, I'll remember what it felt like to be a kid. What is it about adults that makes them forget what they felt like when they were our age?"

We all giggled, and Lia seemed to relax a little.

"Can I try it?" Sheila asked eagerly, pointing at the device. "The mindreading app?"

"I guess," the girl replied uncertainly.

"Wait, but you haven't finished telling us your story!" I said.

"Right. So anyway, you made this app, and we were able to use it to find out where they were keeping the device that disabled the medallion. It's a long story, but we managed to sneak into their headquarters and turn off the device, just long enough to use the medallion and get back here."

"And what about me?" I asked, a lump growing in the pit of my stomach. "I mean, my older self."

She looked at me, a grave expression on her face. "You -" She stopped and shook her head. "You -"

My heart skipped a beat. "What? What happened to me?" I gulped and met Sheila's eyes.

"That's just it," the girl said in a soft voice. "You were supposed to come back here with me. I don't know what happened. Maybe they… arrested you." Her voice broke and her eyes welled up with tears. "The Privileged, they've turned the world into an awful, dark and dreary place. And the worst part is, nobody seems to care. Everyone's gotten used to it, and in school we even learn that that's how things are supposed to be!"

I reached into a basket of stuff on the clubhouse floor and pulled out a small box of tissues. "Here," I said, giving one to the girl. "Don't worry. Now that you're here, I'm sure we'll find some way of fixing this."

"Hey, wait a minute!" Sheila suddenly said, jumping up. "Janie, didn't that note we got from your older self say that there can be only one of a person at any given place and time? Maybe that's why she never came – because if she did, you couldn't be here!"

"Yeah, I remember that," I murmured. I turned to Lia. "Why did you decide to come *here*? I mean, I definitely want to help you, but

I'm still just a kid! Why didn't you find me ten years from now, or twenty?"

"It was you. You said that when you were eleven you were the most creative you've ever been in your life, and that you'd probably have some great ideas." Then her voice grew quiet as something seemed to dawn on her. "She *knew* she wouldn't make it back here. She wanted us to speak to you, and she knew that if she came, you'd disappear or something."

My mind was reeling. My older self, who had *made a mindreading app*, thought I was more creative *now*? And thought it made sense to put the future of the world in the hands of an eleven year old girl? I thought of my mom, who always goes on about how great things were when she was little. I guess that's just another part of grown-ups not really remembering what it's really like to be a kid.

Just then, there was a knock on the clubhouse door.

"Come in!" I said automatically, regretting my words immediately. The last thing we needed was for anyone to see us with Lia.

The door pushed open, and someone poked their head in. I glanced up at them and my stomach did a flip-flop.

Marcia.

******

"Hi guys!" Marcia said cheerily, sitting down on the floor next to us. "Your mom said it was ok for me to come out here. What are you guys doing?" She seemed to have just noticed the girl, and was looking her up and down with a barely-concealed sneer.

"Who are you?" she asked brusquely.

I shot Sheila a nervous glance, and she cleared her throat. "She's, um, my cousin. From Milwaukee. Her name is Sheila too, but everybody calls her Lia. We're both, uh, named after the same aunt." She added lamely.

Lia raised an eyebrow at Sheila, but didn't say anything. I noticed she was clutching her device more tightly now, and seemed to be pointing it in Marcia's direction.

I couldn't believe our rotten luck. Of all the people I least wanted to see right now, Marcia was probably at the very top of the list. What the heck was she doing here now, of all times? Did she know…?

Before the thought could even form in my mind, I saw Lia go pale and start shaking with fear. She pointed a trembling hand at Marcia. "S-s-she. I-i-it's…" It seemed like she couldn't even get the words out.

The next thing I knew, Lia had grabbed Sheila's and my hands and blurted out, "June 10, 2071! June 10, 2071! June 10, 2071!" The medallion, which she must have taken out of her pocket, glinted sharply in the sunlight that came in through the clubhouse window.

And the last thing I saw, before we plunged into the tunnel, was Marcia holding firmly on to my shoulder.

******

We screamed as we fell through the tunnel, landing with a thud on what felt like a huge slab of cement. I gasped and looked around frantically, feeling like I'd had the wind knocked out of me, and tried to catch my breath. Sheila was sitting next to me, looking dazed, but Lia had already stood up and was brushing herself off.

And what I saw next nearly made me fall over. Marcia was sprawled out on the cement beside me, an astonished look on her face. Somehow, she had managed to come along for the ride.

"W-w-what was that?" she asked in a quavering voice.

I just sat there, speechless. I had no idea what Lia was planning, and I certainly didn't know what to say to Marcia. Had she come with us on purpose? Or did she just get swept along by mistake?

Her designer jeans were ripped at the knee and small drops of blood had begun gathering along the tear. She must have seen me staring, because she looked down at her pants and gave a little jump. "What h-happened?" she sputtered. "W-where are we?"

By then Sheila had recovered, and she stood up and walked towards Marcia, her eyes narrowed suspiciously. "You came here on purpose, didn't you!" she said.

"C-came w-w-where?" Marcia's eyes were wide, and she looked genuinely terrified.

"Come on, who do you think you're kidding?" Sheila demanded, crossing her arms and looking down at Marcia angrily. "We know you stole Janie's medallion! Why are you acting all clueless?"

At that, Marcia burst into tears, and she looked so pitiful that I almost felt sorry for her.

Lia took a few steps forward and pointed at Marcia. "You're Marcia Wright, aren't you? Jackie Wright's little sister?" She said it like it was an accusation. "You might as well admit it. I know who you are. And I know why you're here."

By now Marcia was hiccupping and taking short, quick breaths to stop herself from crying. Sheila and I exchanged bewildered glances.

"I-I don't have any idea what you're talking about!" Marcia insisted, getting up and wiping her eyes with the back of her hand. She turned to me. "Yes, I took your stupid medallion. But I don't know what it is! It was for my stupid sister. I'm sorry, ok? I just -" She paused and rubbed her knee. "Will someone please tell me what the heck is going on here?"

I pursed my lips. I wanted to believe Marcia, but the thing was – she lied a lot.

Even after she stole the medallion, and even after I got it back by sneaking into her sister's room, she pretended like nothing had happened. And it was super suspicious that after years of tormenting me and acting like queen of the world, she suddenly wanted to be my friend. I had figured it was because of everything that happened with Kellie. But what if it really had to do with the medallion?

Sheila faced Marcia with her hands on her hips. "Well, Marcia, we just travelled through time, and we're in the year 2071. Lia here is from the future and it turns out she's Janie's granddaughter."

I stifled a laugh. Nothing like beating around the bush.

Marica stared at Sheila, her mouth hanging open. I had to hand it to her. Either she was a really, really good actress, or she honestly had no clue what was happening.

"Janie, Sheila – I have to talk to you." Lia cast a pointed look in Marcia's direction. "ALONE."

We huddled together and Lia leaned in towards us and whispered anxiously, "I should have known Marcia would be lurking around you guys." She shook her head. "This is bad news. REALLY bad news."

"Why?" Sheila asked, forgetting to whisper. I elbowed her and she lowered her voice. "Sorry. I mean – why?" she whispered.

"Her sister, Jackie, is one of the leaders of the Protectors of Fate!" Lia exclaimed. "She was instrumental in the takeover of the Privileged, and after they came to power, they appointed her Governor of Middleton." Lia shuddered and readjusted her thick glasses. "She's one of the Chief Enforcers of the Code of Behavior."

"The Code of Behavior?" Sheila interjected.

Lia nodded. "The Privileged enforce the Code ruthlessly. We

learn it every day in school and we are expected to follow it at all times!"

"What does the Code say?" I asked. It sounded weird, like something out of an adventure video game.

She gestured to her strange clothing. "Well, for one thing, everyone has to dress like this. And we're not supposed to make ourselves look pretty. The Privileged say that beauty just distracts people from important things, like work and school."

"Do they make you wear your hair like that too?" Sheila asked.

Lia looked startled. "What's wrong with my hair?" she demanded.

"Uh…" Sheila flushed and looked horrified. "I'm sorry, I just -" Then she recovered. "I guess we're just used to different styles, that's all."

After a few tense moments, the girl grinned. "Hey, I wouldn't be caught dead with your old-fashioned hairdos." We all giggled.

Surreal didn't even *begin* to describe this conversation.

I leaned over and whispered to Sheila, "Open mouth, insert foot."

She chuckled. "Hey, it's not my fault she wears her hair like that!"

"We also have to wear these." Lia took off her thick, brown glasses and held them up for us to see. "*All the time.*"

"What are they?" Sheila looked intrigued.

"MG's," Lia said. "Monitor Glasses. The Privileged use them to keep track of people, listen to their conversations, and send messages to people when they want to."

Sheila looked shocked. "So they can hear us right now?"

Lia shook her head. "No." She lowered her voice and looked around again.Luckily there was no one in sight, except a very forlorn Marcia, who was sitting on the pavement and rocking back and forth, hugging her knees to her chest. "We've figured out how to take apart their monitoring system for short periods of time. But anyone who is caught without their MG's can be arrested and -" She shuddered involuntarily. "Rescripted."

Rescripted? Whatever that was, it definitely didn't sound good.

I opened my mouth to ask, but before I could say anything, Lia put her hand up. "I don't have time to explain everything now." She fished around in her big, ugly brown bag and pulled out two more pairs of glasses. "Here, put these on, quick."

I took the glasses from her and slipped them on gingerly, gathering my hair away from my face. I closed my eyes tightly, expecting things to look all blurry when I opened them, but I was surprised to find that if anything, things looked *clearer* than they usually did.

"Hey!" Sheila whispered. "I can see better with these on!"

"That's because they automatically adjust to your eyesight," Lia said. She said it like it was the most natural thing in the world.

"Wow," Sheila said. "I can even see each of the little leaves on the tree over there!"

Lia snorted. "Maybe you should get your eyes checked." She rummaged around in her bag again and pulled out some clothes like the ones she was wearing. "Put these on too," she said. "You've got to blend in."

Sheila gawked at the dark navy leggings and orange tunics Lia shoved at us. "You can't really expect us to wear these," she protested. "They're huge!"

I frowned at Sheila. "Seriously? You're worried about *fashion* at a time like this?" I met Lia's eyes and shook my head, grinning.

"Hey!" Sheila said indignantly, "Just because you don't care about clothes and stuff, doesn't mean I shouldn't. And anyway, all I meant was – they're so big, they'll fall right off of us!"

"Just put them on," Lia said, obviously making an effort to be patient. "They'll adjust to your size automatically."

Sheila shrugged and we pulled the strange clothes on over our jeans and tee-shirts. Sure enough, they fit both us perfectly. And strangely, it didn't even feel like I was wearing two layers of clothing. In fact, these were probably the most comfortable clothes I'd ever worn. They felt silky and flexible, and didn't press into my skin the way my jeans did sometimes.

I took a deep breath, and for the first time tried to take calm inventory of our surroundings. We were in what looked like a large empty parking lot, except that there were no spaces marked for cars. I could see some buildings off in the distance, but except for that, it was cement as far as the eye could see. It was quiet – almost too quiet – and I thought back to the time we had visited 1739. It felt kind of like that – There didn't seem to be any *background noise*. And something else was bothering me, something I couldn't quite put my finger on.

Sheila broke into my thoughts. "What about her?" she jerked her thumb in Marcia's direction. "Doesn't she need glasses? And clothes?"

Lia shrugged. "I wasn't expecting her. She'll just have to take her chances."

"Well…." I paused for a moment. "What exactly are we here for? Do you have a plan?"

Lia looked surprised. "No," she said, running a hand through her wild hair. "You're the legendary Janie Ray." She focused her gaze on me. "I was kind of hoping you'd come up with something."

******

Me? Legendary? Even after all we'd been through, it was kind of impossible for me to imagine a world in which I was some kind of hero. And why was my older self so convinced I could figure everything out? My mind was racing. I kicked the ground with my sneaker and tried to slow down my thoughts. I needed to calm down and think logically about everything that was happening.

Lia had told us that the medallion had stopped working twenty-five years before she took her little trip to our time. I did a quick calculation in my head. *That would be 2046.* Why had Lia taken us back *here* to 2071, when the Privileged were already in power? What we *should* have done was go back to 2046 and prevent them from disabling the medallion in the first place. And now – My blood ran cold. She had said the medallion *didn't even work here.* How would we ever get home?

I hadn't seen Lia pointing her little tablet at me, but she must have read my mind, because she smiled and said, "You have *your* medallion in your pocket, right? Your older self said that you carry it around with you everywhere you go." She yanked her chin in Marcia's direction. "Especially since *she* tried to steal it. It should work fine here. At least that's what *you* told me."

I reached under the tunic and stuffed my hand in my jeans pocket, exhaling with relief when I felt the cool touch of the medallion.

"I just came back here kind of automatically," Lia explained apologetically. "I guess I panicked when I saw Marcia. And I was worried about you. I mean, your older self. Obviously, you're right though. If we go back and fix things in 2046, your older self will never be arrested in the first place. If that's what happened."

Sheila spoke up then. "Ok, so then we have a plan! We'll use Janie's medallion to get back to 2046 and set things right."

I nodded. "Just one thing. Can you stop saying *your older self?* It kind of creeps me out. How about we just call her Prof. Ray. After all – she's not really me, is she? I mean, at least not yet."

Lia smiled. "No problem," she said. "As long as I don't have to call you Grandma."

******

"Come on Marcia," I said, waving her over with my hand. We're going now."

Marcia looked up at me, a blank look in her eyes. I think she was shell-shocked.

"You're not seriously thinking of taking her with us!" Lia said forcefully. "Janie, you have no idea what she's done! She's been her sister's helper all her life, and she's completely on the side of the Privileged. She's been totally brainwashed!" She narrowed her eyes. "She's probably a spy."

I crossed my arms stubbornly. "You mean what she *will* do in the future! We don't actually *know* how involved she is at this point. If she's a spy we'll deal with it. But there is no *way* I'm leaving her here!" Marcia was a big pain in the neck, and I didn't trust her, but I wasn't ready to abandon her to some horrible fate.

And there was another thing. I refused to believe the future was set in stone. Maybe Marcia came out like that in one possible future. But as long as we could get back home, there was still a chance she wouldn't!

Lia didn't look convinced, but Sheila put her hand on my shoulder. "I'm with Janie," she said quietly. "Marcia comes."

We must have been pretty engrossed in our argument, because

when I turned again to tell Marcia to hurry it up, I saw something that made my hair stand on end.

We weren't alone anymore.

A group of kids was headed our way, and they were already just a few feet away from where Marcia was now standing on wobbly legs.

"It's your turn!" a girl said, a smile on her face. There were five of them, and they were all dressed exactly alike, in the same navy leggings and orange tunics we were wearing. They practically looked like clones of one another. Even their haircuts were almost identical. And since the thick brown glasses hid much of their faces, it was almost impossible to tell them apart.

"Ok," another one said. I was pretty sure this one was a boy. He was a bit taller than the others, and his face was full of zits. "I'm going to count to 100!" An excited titter went through the group. Their strange laughter made them sound like a flock of little birds.

It was then that they noticed Marcia, standing in full view on the sidewalk, in normal 2011 clothes and no special glasses.

In an instant, before I could react, they had surrounded her. "She is not wearing her MG's," one of them said. Her voice had taken on a robotic quality.

"And she is not dressed according to Code," another one added.

"We must call the Enforcers," a third one said. He spoke in a flat tone, as if he were talking about the weather or something equally uninteresting.

As the panic rose in my throat, I was struck by how unemotional they seemed about the whole thing. A few minutes ago they had been laughing and talking almost like normal people – even if their game sounded kind of weird. But now they were acting like bizarre *automatons*. Like they had been programmed to react in a certain way.

All at once, their glasses started flashing and beeping. They had already locked arms, forming a tight ring around Marcia, and there didn't seem to be any way to break through. I grabbed on to Sheila's hand and squeezed. Now what?

"Janie, we have to go now," Lia said urgently. "I understand you want to help Marcia, and that's really kind of you. But there's nothing we can do. People here are trained from the time they're little kids to report Code Breakers, and once a ring like that has been formed, it's impossible to break into it. Trust me, people have tried. And it just can't be done."

I met Sheila's eyes and she offered an encouraging smile. Emboldened, I turned back to Lia. "I'm sorry, Lia," I said, slipping my medallion back into my pocket. "But that's just not an option. We're going to have to figure out another way."

Lia shook her head sadly. "You're taking a big risk, Janie," she said resignedly. "I just hope you know what you're doing."

"Well, don't get your hopes up," I said, sighing loudly. "I don't have a clue."

At that very moment, another group of people appeared out of nowhere. I can't really describe them, except to say that they looked kind of like the Robocop cartoons RJ watches. They were huge, with thick metal armor and masks on their faces. My heart stopped and I took a step back, grasping Sheila's quivering hand for dear life.

The Robocop people didn't say anything, and within moments they were gone. It was as if they had disappeared into thin air.

And they had taken Marcia with them.

******

I sank back down on the pavement and put my head between my knees. I was starting to get a splitting headache.

"Ok, genius," Lia said, slumping down next to me. "What do we do now?"

I didn't answer, and instead rubbed my temples, trying to clear my thoughts.

"Look, getting nasty is going to get us nowhere," Sheila said, looking pointedly at Lia. "We're in this together."

After a slight pause, Lia relented. "Ok, you're right. Sorry." Then she brightened. "Actually, I have an idea!"

"What is it?" Sheila asked excitedly.

Lia stood up and motioned for us to follow. "We have to find the

Outer Circle. Just come with me and stay quiet. Walk with your head down, look serious, and whatever you do – don't say or do anything to stand out."

******

We had been walking for several minutes when we reached a street with buildings and well-manicured trees lining the sides. It looked like your average Main Street in any regular town, with stores and restaurants and stuff like that. Except there were still no cars. And the street was full of pedestrians, all dressed like us, walking together in small, quiet groups.

I looked at one of the trees as we passed by, and with a jolt I realized what had been bothering me earlier. *The trees were fake.* I reached out to touch one, but Lia caught my hand and gave me a warning glance. "You don't want to do that," she said sternly. "Like I said. Don't do anything unusual."

I pulled my hand back and bit my lip. It was unusual to touch the trees? Then something else struck me. There wasn't any grass, either. Even the fake trees were completely surrounded by cement.

"Why isn't there any grass?" I whispered to Lia. "And why aren't the trees real?'

"The Code requires all public spaces to be perfectly neat," Lia said. "The Privileged don't approve of plants," she added. "They think they're too messy."

I considered this. "But there's still one thing I don't understand.

Why does everybody go along with this stuff? I mean, why do they agree to be controlled like that?"

Lia made a face. "You have to remember how the Privileged came to power. Once they disabled the medallion, all they had to do was wait for an opportunity to grab control. In 2051 there was a horrible Plague that made half the people in the world sick. Lots and lots of people died, and things were in chaos. The Privileged stepped in and took charge of the situation. They helped lots of people get better, and at first everyone thought they were really great. Gradually, they managed to convince people that giving them power was the only way to stay safe. I guess when people are scared, they'll be willing to give up almost anything to protect themselves and their families.

"Nowadays, people don't even remember how things were before. They're just used to it, you know? They don't know any other reality. And they are taught to believe that control by the Privileged is the only way to keep things from going crazy again." She looked me in the eyes. "And you have to understand. Lots of people think they have good lives, even now. They don't even realize what they're missing. The only reason I do is because of you." She chuckled softly. "I mean, Prof. Ray. Even my parents don't really understand."

Just then a large poster on one of the nearby buildings caught my eye, and I stopped short, drawing in a sharp breath.

The poster showed the portrait of an old lady, with steel eyes and a determined look on her face. Underneath the picture it said, "Here to Protect You". A shiver went up my spine. She had aged, but I had no doubt in mind who it was.

******

"You see!" Lia whispered in an I-told-you-so voice, as she prodded me to keep walking. "That's her! That's Marcia's sister."

I gulped and nodded, trying to take it all in.

"Just look back down at the ground," Lia said, "and don't slow down. We're almost there."

I glanced over at Sheila, who hadn't said anything the entire time, and saw her carefully studying the pavement. I wondered if she had overheard our conversation, or whether she was lost in her own thoughts.

A few seconds later Lia stopped in front of a large gray building with a tall wooden door. "We're here," she whispered. She knocked three times, paused slightly and then knocked twice more. I heard a rustling from inside, and then a man opened the door just a crack. He peeked out, and when he saw Lia, he smiled and moved aside to let us in.

"You're here." The man breathed a sigh of relief. "We could tell something was happening, but we weren't sure exactly what."

He faced me and Sheila and stuck out his hand. "You must be Janie. And you're Sheila. I'm -"

"You're Michael Walleger's son!" Sheila cut him off. He was tall and had the same sharp, blue eyes and thinning hair that Michael did.

The man looked impressed, and his eyes twinkled. "Yup, guilty as charged. Jeremy Walleger. Nice to meet you."

"I – I'm sorry about your father. Passing away, I mean," I said.

"Yes, thank you. It's been several years since he died, but I still miss him every day." He gave Lia a questioning look. "Did anyone follow you?"

She shook her head. "No, I don't think so."

"Ok then. Come with me." Without even waiting for a reply, he started walking down a long corridor, and we followed him into a large room with big metal doors. "This is a safe room," he explained. "It's specially designed to avoid monitoring by the Privileged. We can talk freely here."

The room was huge – even bigger than I had realized – and it was lined with hundreds of shelves stuffed with all kinds of things. It looked almost like a warehouse.

Sheila nudged me. "Look at that!" She pointed at a shelf that had rows and rows of toys on it. "Cool!" Another shelf was full of old books, and another one seemed to be packed with make-up and stuff like that. What looked like a huge computer stood in the corner, whirring and making occasional clicking sounds.

"This is the Collection," Jeremy explained, sitting down on a large, plush chair in the center of the room. We sat down on smaller chairs next to him. "It's where we keep all the things the

Privileged have forbidden. Books, games and stuff like that." He indicated the big computer. "That's where we keep digital stuff. Like music, movies, TV shows and that kind of thing. And we have a copy of all the information that's ever been on the internet."

"People aren't allowed to watch TV anymore? And there's no more internet?" Sheila asked. I swear, I think that upset her more than seeing those Robocop guys.

"Nope. They want people to get all their information from their glasses. Plus," he grimaced, "they don't believe in entertainment."

"So, Jeremy," Lia began. "We're in a bit of trouble." *Understatement of the year, anyone?*

After Lia had explained what happened, Jeremy leaned back in his chair and regarded me admiringly. "Good for you, Janie," he said. "You did the right thing by refusing to abandon Marcia. You may still be a kid, but you're every bit as determined as the Janie Ray I know."

Lia looked uncomfortable, and I avoided her eyes.

"Anyway," he continued thoughtfully. "It's pretty clear where they took her." He opened a small drawer on one of the shelves and pulled out a small map, spreading it out on the floor beside us. "Here. At Headquarters."

"Ok, so can we just use your teleporter thingie to go there and get Marcia?" Sheila asked.

Jeremy shook his head. "I wish it were that simple. We've figured out how to prevent them from monitoring us – not all the time, mind you, but long enough to get things done, when we need to. But we can't use the teleporter without them tracking it."

"Oh, so that explains why we walked here," I said. "How hard is it to sneak into Headquarters? They probably have it pretty well guarded." I thought of those weird Robocop guys and my stomach turned over.

"Actually, not really," Jeremy said. "They rely pretty heavily on electronic monitoring. They have no idea we've figured out how to block it. Plus, we have the Mindreader app and they don't know a thing about that. You can use it to figure out when the coast is clear, and then just sneak in. Since you won't show up on their electronic screening, they might not give you a second thought."

"That sounds like it's easier said than done," I said, trying to conceal the tremor in my voice.

"It is," Lia agreed. "But it's not impossible. And we don't have any time to lose."

As we got up to leave, my stomach grumbled loudly, and I realized I hadn't eaten for hours. I was incredibly nervous, but I guess even nervous people have to eat. Jeremy must have heard it, because he reached up and grabbed something from one of the shelves.

"This isn't very good, but it'll do the job," he said. He popped open a can and handed us each something that looked like a biscuit. "It tastes like cardboard, but it has all the nutrients you need, and exactly the right number of calories for a meal."

I was so famished, I'd have gobbled it up even if it tasted like Brussel sprouts. I finished it in a few quick bites and brushed the crumbs off my lips. It actually wasn't half bad.

"Good luck," Jeremy said, leading us to the door and holding it open. "This won't be easy, but I have full confidence in you."

I turned and waved goodbye, but the door had closed, and he was gone.

******

We walked in silence for several blocks before Lia whispered, "It's coming up on our left." A few moments later we stopped in front of a large, gray building, very much like all the other ones, except even bigger. It must have been at least fifteen stories tall, and it stretched all the way down to the next block.

"You snuck in here before," Sheila said to Lia in a low voice. "Do you know where they're holding her?"

"Not exactly, but I do have an idea of where to start looking. Just keep your heads down and follow me." She held out her device and waited. Then she motioned for us to start walking. "There's no one here. The Mindreader isn't picking anything up. This is our chance!"

We walked hurriedly, single file, and I concentrated all my energy on trying to be as inconspicuous as possible. I had lost my scrunchie at some point on the way to Jeremy's, but I figured that was probably a good thing – wild hair seemed to be "in" around here.

"Can you use the Mindreader to find Marcia?" I asked. "I mean, search for her particular thoughts and zero in on where they're coming from?"

"Hmm, that's an interesting idea," Lia murmured. "I hadn't thought of it. It should work, though." She tapped on her screen and quickly typed something in. Then she held it up and waited. It beeped softly and she beamed. "Yup, we've got her. Third floor, second door on the right."

"Hold on," Sheila said, looking nervous. "What do we do when we find her?"

"We wait until the right moment, and then run inside, grab her hand and use the medallion." Lia explained matter-of-factly. "The only question is -"

"What?" I asked, wiping my palms on my tunic. I was so nervous, even my hands were sweating.

"Where do we go? Back to 2046? Or -"

"Leave that to me," I said, a plan starting to take form in my mind. "Just lead us to Marcia, and I'll take it from there."

******

A few seconds later we found a staircase and walked up to the second floor. It was incredible how easy it was to walk around this place that was supposedly so well protected. They were so confident they had everyone under their thumb, it never even occurred to them that someone would sneak in undetected.

We started down the hallway, and almost immediately I could hear Marcia's voice from down the corridor. "You've got it all wrong!" she was saying. I wondered who she was talking to.

"Come in here, guys!" I slipped into an empty room adjacent to the one Marcia was in. "Somebody's with her."

We stood stiffly up against the wall, trying to position ourselves so that anyone passing by wouldn't see us. I kept my ear pressed against the wall, trying to hear what was going on in the next room.

"I'm ashamed," a low voice was saying. "I don't know who you are, or why your DNA matches my grandma's, but you're *nothing* like her. Marcia Wright, my grandmother, worked her whole life to make this place possible, to help people live more orderly lives. She's always been proud to serve the Privileged and to be Jackie Wright's loyal assistant!"

I looked at Sheila, and she stared back at me with wide eyes. I guess I wasn't the only one who was having a little run in with their granddaughter.

"Proud? How could anyone be proud of all this horribleness?" Marcia cried. "This place is awful! It's – horrifying! You have everyone under your thumbs, like little robots. Everybody's the same, and nobody can think for themselves!"

Sheila nudged me, unable to resist a small grin. "I never thought I'd see the day when *Marcia* would give such an impassioned speech against conforming."

I snickered. That was for sure.

In the next room, Marcia was still talking. "You can tell yourselves that you're doing it for people's own good. But we both know that's a lie! You just want to stay in power!"

"That's absurd," the low voice said. "But there's really no point in continuing this discussion. I'll be back in two minutes, and we'll begin the Rescripting. Once that's done, you won't even remember any of this, and everything will be just fine."

I tapped Lia on the shoulder. "There's that word again!" I said. "What is this Rescripting business?"

"It's the Privileged's ultimate weapon of control," Lia said. "When all else fails, they erase a person's memory and reset their frame of mind. That way -"

But I had heard enough. I stood up and headed for the door, motioning for Lia and Sheila to follow. It was time to leave.

******

We tiptoed out of the room as quietly as we could and I poked my head into Marcia's room, breathing a sigh of relief when I saw she was alone.

"This is it guys, come on!" I ran over to Marcia and gave her a big hug. I held her hand, grasping the medallion between my fingers, and reached out to grab onto Sheila and Lia.

"Janie!" Marcia cried. "I'm so sorry! I can't believe I was a part of this. And I can't believe Jackie was either! We've got to figure out a way to

fix this. Like maybe with time travel?" She looked at me hopefully. "I can't just go home and let this horrible future happen!"

"You don't have to," I whispered. "Your future is up to you."

She nodded. I knew she wouldn't remember any of this when we got back home, but I hoped that this experience would leave its mark, just enough so that she could choose a different path.

I looked up and was horrified to see a group of Enforcers approaching the door.

"Stop them!" one of them shouted as they burst into the room.

There was no time to lose. "May 19, 2011! My 19, 2011! May 19, 2011!" I cried.

And with that we disappeared, leaving a very confused and very angry group of Enforcers in our wake.

******

♥ May 20, 2011 ♥

Dear Diary,

Sorry for leaving you hanging yesterday – but my hand was killing me!! I think that might have been my longest diary entry yet!

Anyway, what happened next was this:

We landed back in the clubhouse, piled on top of one another.

"Ouch!" I said, pulling my arm out from under Sheila's head.

"Tell me about it!" she complained, sitting up and moving Lia's big, brown bag off her leg. "We really have to work on our landing."

Lia, Sheila and I stood up slowly, and only Marcia remained lying on the floor, snoring loudly.

"So what now?" Lia asked, looking at me expectantly. "Do we go to 2046 now and stop them from disabling the medallion?"

"If so, I have to pee first," Sheila said.

I grinned. "Nah, actually I'm hoping we won't have to do that."

Lia looked puzzled. "Why not?"

A small smile played at my lips. "Well, let's just see what happens when Marcia wakes up."

At that, Marcia stirred and started to sit up. She was holding onto her head and making a terrible face. "What happened?" she asked, looking around the clubhouse. She seemed pretty confused.

"Nothing, you just hit your head," I said gently. "You're fine. Do you want some lemonade?"

The glasses of lemonade we'd been drinking before our trip were still there on the clubhouse floor. We hadn't even knocked them over with our clumsy landing!

"Sure," she murmured. She picked up one of the glasses and took a long drink. When she put it down, she smiled warmly at Lia. "I'm sorry, I don't remember your name. You're Sheila's cousin from Milwaukee, right?"

"Uh… yeah," Lia said, sticking out her hand and smiling back. "Nice to meet you." I guess even Lia was convinced this Marcia wasn't the same one she knew in the future. At least not yet.

I heard the sound of a bird chirping really loudly, and Marcia reached into her pocket and pulled out her cell phone. "Ugh, it's my sister," she said, rolling her eyes. "What does she want now?"

"Yes, Jackie, what is it? I'm in the middle of -" There was a short silence and then "No, Jackie, I will not do that for you. Just because you're in college doesn't mean you get to boss me around! And don't get me mixed up in all your stuff, Jackie. I don't like it. Not one bit!" Without waiting for an answer she slammed her cell phone down on the clubhouse floor and closed her eyes.

"You go, girl!" I said, putting my arm around Marcia's shoulder. I winked at Sheila and Lia. I had a feeling everything was going to be just fine.

******

Twenty minutes later, Marcia had gone home, and as we carried the lemonade glasses into the kitchen, I spotted a pink note sticking out from under the microwave.

I picked up, and sure enough it was written in our secret language. After Sheila had deciphered it, I looked up and met Lia's eyes. "It's over," I said. "We don't have to go to 2046, after all."

"Why not?" Lia asked. "How can you be sure?"

"Well, let's just say Janie here wrote herself a little note," Sheila chuckled. "It would seem a certain Professor Janie Ray from the year 2071 paid us a visit to let us know that everything worked out."

"It did?" Lia looked bewildered.

"Look, I'm not into grandmotherly speeches, but there is one thing I want you to remember. No matter how bad things get, we can choose our own future." I reached over and pinched Lia's cheek with a wry smile.

Lia grinned. "Are you going to tell me how much I've grown now?"

I giggled. "Nope. But I am going to miss you, kiddo."

*****

♥ May 21, 2011 ♥

Dear Diary,

So that's the whole story. Lia went back home to a whole new reality. And it looks like some things will be changing around here, too.

Oh, and tonight was the awesomest night EVER. Remember how weird Sheila and Alexis were acting when Kellie said she was planning to take her parents out for a fancy dinner to celebrate the whole Starbright thing?

Well, it turns out that was because the fancy dinner was a surprise party for *me*!

Kellie planned the whole thing, and even got my parents' permission and everything. My dad said we were going out to dinner as a family, and we drove to Marty's – one of my absolute FAVORITE restaurants. They have an all-you-can-eat kids' menu, with great pizza, spaghetti and stuff like that. And I hate to admit it, but I still love the little prizes you get with the kids' meal.

Anyway, when we got to the restaurant, Kellie and her parents were waiting for us, along with Alexis, Sheila and even Marcia.

"I couldn't have done it without you," Kellie said as I sat down next to her. "I just wanted to say thank you. You're an amazing friend." She reached over and gave me a hug.

"So are you," I replied, a warm glow settling over me. "I don't know what I would do without friends like you guys."

****

THE END

♥ Janie and Sheila's Secret Language ♥

(Just switch each letter of the alphabet with the secret letter underneath it):

A	B	C	D	E	F	G	H	I	J
o	h	r	m	i	q	n	k	e	p
K	L	M	N	O	P	Q	R	S	T
g	d	t	s	u	w	v	z	l	j
U	V	W	X	Y	Z				
a	x	f	b	y	c				

Made in the USA
Lexington, KY
06 December 2017